William Black

Wolfenberg

Vol. I.

William Black

Wolfenberg
Vol. I.

ISBN/EAN: 9783337044800

Printed in Europe, USA, Canada, Australia, Japan

Cover: Foto ©Andreas Hilbeck / pixelio.de

More available books at **www.hansebooks.com**

WOLFENBERG

BY

WILLIAM BLACK

IN THREE VOLUMES.

VOL. I.

LONDON:

SAMPSON LOW, MARSTON & COMPANY

LIMITED,

St. Dunstan's House,

FETTER LANE, FLEET STREET, E.C.

1892.

LONDON:
PRINTED BY WILLIAM CLOWES AND SONS, LIMITED,
STAMFORD STREET AND CHARING CROSS.

[' *Of Poseidon, the mighty God, I begin my lay, Poseidon who shakes the earth and the sea unharvested, God of the deep, who possesses Helicon and wide Aegae. A double honour have the Gods given thee, oh Earthshaker, to be at once the tamer of steeds and the saviour of ships. Then hail, Poseidon, the girdler of the world, the dark-haired deity; and do thou, oh Blessed one, keep a kindly heart, and succour seafaring men.'—A.L.*]

CONTENTS OF VOL. I.

CHAPTER   PAGE

I. FORTUITOUS ATOMS 1

II. TWO DISCOVERIES 27

III. A DEVIATION 51

IV. AN INTRODUCTION ... 77

V. A HOROSCOPE 103

VI. " VIX E CONSPECTU SICULÆ TELLURIS " 131

VII. THE EAR OF DIONYSIUS 158

VIII. " TO ATHENS SHALL THE LOVERS WEND " 187

IX. FACING CONTINGENCIES ... 216

WOLFENBERG.

CHAPTER I.

FORTUITOUS ATOMS.

WHAT is the space, then, that lies between comedy and tragedy? In this instance, it was merely the breadth of a table in the saloon of the Orient s.s. *Orotania*. For here were we, the most careless and irresponsible set of creatures that ever were shaken into seats by the dice-box of Fate (the Purser); and there were they—— But let us begin at the beginning.

We first noticed them as they were crossing the pier at Tilbury, on their way to the tender. There was an elderly lady, sallow of face,

with silver-white hair beautifully braided.
There was her daughter, a young woman of
about five-and-twenty, of a pale and clear
complexion, with dark and lustrous eyes,
highly-arched black eyebrows, and magnifi-
cently-massed black hair. Then there was
a man apparently about forty-five, of middle
height or something thereunder, with a long
brown moustache, a clipped brown beard, and
a firm and decided mouth that seemed somehow out of keeping with his large, grey,
dreamy eyes. Indeed, he wore something of
an absent look; it was his two companions
who were most alert and interested, especially
the younger lady, who was talking and
laughing with a gay vivacity.

"Peggy," observed a certain small creature
who keeps her own and certain other house-
holds in meek subjection—though now she
spoke with bated breath—"those two are
countrywomen of yours."

"I think you forget which is my country,"

replied Lady Cameron of Inverfask, a little proudly. "But they are Americans, if that is what you mean."

The next moment—the new arrivals were now coming along the gangway—a startling thing occurred. The man's face appeared to undergo a gradual and yet swift transformation. Or was it not rather that this definite and actual, this living and breathing, physiognomy summoned up all sorts of ghosts— outlined portraits in the illustrated papers— perhaps, even, some likeness in oil in this or that exhibition? One had certainly seen those features before—in books, or magazines, or weekly journals. Then a hasty and furtive appeal to the printed list of passengers, and the mystery was solved at once: this was no other than Wolfenberg, the great American artist—the most imaginative painter that America has yet produced—the painter of dreams and visions, of phantasms and mysteries—the painter of "The Return of

Undine," of "Two Lovers in a Valley in the Moon," of "The Goddess Athene Entering the Chamber of Nausicaa." Our souls rejoiced over the discovery; it was something even to be sailing in the same vessel with this master of the magic wand, this compeller of clouds and tempests, this traveller who had been through the spirit-worlds, whose eyes had beheld strange things.

And when our good fortune (or the Purser) so arranged affairs that we found ourselves seated opposite these three in the saloon of the great steamer, an acquaintanceship was struck up at once; that is easily managed on board ship; the passing of a salt-cellar will suffice. Of course it was the young lady who at the outset demanded most attention, and seemed to expect it, and got it. For one thing, there was no unnecessary shyness about her; she was eagerly interested in everything around her; she chatted freely, smiling and showing pretty teeth, sometimes laughing merrily with her lustrous black eyes. Moreover, she was pleasant to look at. If she was not strictly beautiful, there was at least something curiously seductive in her appearance—something striking, too, in the contrast between the magnificent black hair and the pale skin and red lips. Perhaps that unusually bright crimson owed a little to artifice, or was it merely accentuated by the prevailing pallor of her complexion? At all events, her pallor was not the pallor of an invalid. There was not much of the invalid about Amélie Dumaresq, as we subsequently discovered her name to be. To us, who were no further away from her than the breadth of the table, she seemed literally to thrill to the finger-tips with life, and with the delight of life. It would have been an almost aggressive vitality had it not been modified by the young lady's evident and placid expectation that she should be listened to, and petted, and made much of. And how patiently her two companions bore with her wilfulness, and her blunt, frank speeches, and her petulant paradoxes. Sometimes, it is true, a cloud came over Wolfenberg's thoughtful and rather tired-looking face : it was as if he would have said, 'Amélie, have a little moderation, before strangers.' But ever and always he skilfully interposed, apologising for her, defending her, explaining that, after all, there was something in what she maintained. His devotion to her, his gentle government of her, his pride in her even when she was most audacious, were all beautiful to witness. So that we congratulated ourselves on this our setting out. There was one table, at least, in the big saloon that promised to be anything but dull.

We lost sight of them after luncheon, for each and all of us went our several ways to arrange cabins, and open trunks, and make preparations for the long seven weeks' voyage. When we saw them again on deck, the day was dying out in crimson flame, with Dover Castle looming large and high and dark against the west; while along the south-eastern horizon lay one massive cloud, vast, portentous, suffused with a sultry light, and dwarfing into insignificance the pale golden-white line of the French coast immediately underneath it. Then by and by the tinkle of the steward's bell was heard all over the ship; and presently we were once more seated opposite our newly-found acquaintances — down here in the saloon, that was now all bravely aglow with the electric lamps.

She took away the breath from us in about the very first second.

"I have got one detestable duty done with this afternoon," said she, addressing herself mostly to the two ladies opposite her. "I thought, as we were going to Greece, I ought to read the Iliad; and I've been struggling with it for days; and, thank goodness, I've finished it at last!"

"Yes?" said our Mrs. Threepenny-bit, with kind inquiry.

"You want to know what I think of it?" said this young person, the contour of whose satin-soft cheek and the liquid splendour of whose dark eyes would not have led one to anticipate the ruthless iconoclasm of her mind. "I think it is absolute trash. I always suspected that Homer was rubbish, and now I know it. And I'll tell you how I suspected it: it was because whenever you found any one writing about Homer and his knowledge of human nature, the one thing that was always dragged in was the parting of Hector and Andromache; and I formed a kind of notion that it was the only bit of human nature in the whole book—the only sample they could show. The Iliad?—it seems to me nothing but the doings and sayings of a lot of great, brawling, boasting prizefighters. The only human beings in it are the immortals— and they are a parcel of big babies."

And so she went on; but one of us seemed to hear no more—seemed rather to be recalling a picture that appeared in the Salon some ten or a dozen years ago. The title of it was, 'Achilles invoking the aid of Thetis;' the subject was the grief-laden hero down by the seashore, stretching out his hands, and imploring his goddess-mother beneath the waves to hear him. This is the passage, according to a recent version: 'So spake he weeping, and his lady mother heard him as she sate in the sea-depths beside her aged sire. With speed arose she from the grey sea, like a mist, and sate her before the face of her weeping son, and stroked him with her hand, and spake and called on his name.' Now that picture was signed 'Ernest Wolfenberg;' and all the artistic circles of Europe were talking of the young American painter who had so boldly carried modern methods, and the dreams of his own high-strung imagination, into the region of classic myth. And did this girl—

whom he seemed absolutely to worship—did
she alone forget ?   Or did she consider (which
is a more charitable view) that his position as
a painter was so assured, and his choice of
subject so unerring and indisputable, that
anything she might say about either Art or
Literature was not of much consequence, so
far as their personal relations were concerned ?
None the less did he now come to her aid ;
tried to show that there was something to be
said for her opinion ; and urged the unavoid-
able poverty of translations.   It was pathetic
in its way.   One wondered if it were possible
that she had never even heard of 'Achilles
invoking the aid of Thetis.'

That night we went placidly down Channel,
trying at times to identify the distant streaks
of dull yellow fire with one or other of the
Sussex watering-places.   It was a moonlight
night, calm and still ; a broad band of silver
quivered on the smoothly-undulating sea ; the
throbbing of the engines became a pleasant,

monotonous, drowsy murmur in the silence. At intervals, it is true, we had music on deck; but some of us may have preferred the spaces of quiet; at all events, Peggy—that is to say, Lady Cameron of Inverfask—and her two friends had sought out for themselves a secluded corner aft of the wheel-box; and there whosoever chose could discourse of their shipmates freely. It was of the painter Wolfenberg and of Amélie Dumaresq that one had now to hear.

"Why," said Peggy, after some random observations, "she cannot be more than four or five-and-twenty; and he is getting quite grey !"

"These," responded Mrs. Threepenny-bit, with decision, "are the matches that turn out best—if it is lasting kindness and care that the girl wants."

"She does not seem as devoted to him as he is devoted to her," Peggy went on, in the absent way that is induced when one has a great waste of moonlit water to rest one's eyes on. "But of course she could not show it, especially before strangers. She calls him Ernest, however, and he calls her Amélie, so that it is no ordinary friendship. I wonder, now, if she will marry him for his reputation, his position? Mind you, she has a pretty fair notion of her own importance; don't you think so? She has her own individuality. I doubt whether she would easily take a subordinate place. . . . What exquisite hands she has!"

"And she is aware of it," answered the other, calmly.

"And a very pretty smile—very winning, I think. And a merry laugh, too. Why, she laughs with the laugh of a child!"

"And yet she is an absolute virago in her opinions!" exclaimed the smaller woman, with a touch of amazement. "She is a regular down-with-everythingist, wherever tradition, or custom, or conventionality is concerned."

"At all events," Peggy put in, "she respects convention quite sufficiently in her costume. Both she and her mother are perfectly dressed."

"Peggy, my dear child, anarchical women are never anarchical in their dress—unless through lack of means. And Miss Dumaresq and her mother have just come over from Paris. Didn't you hear? She has been studying in the Atelier Didron, so Mr. Wolfenberg says."

"The girl, you mean?"

"Yes; and she has brought a lot of unfinished work with her. Perhaps, when we become better friends, she may let us have a peep. I confess I am curious—for more than one reason."

And so they talked, and further talked, and speculated, over a subject that seemed to have some mysterious attraction for them; until it was time for us to say good-night and go away to our respective cabins, with one final glance round at the magic world of dark blue-grey and silver-shimmering sea.

Next morning we had a look in at Plymouth; and, just before starting again, Peggy happened to be leaning idly with her arms on the rail, gazing across the green waters of the harbour towards the fair-shining town and its heights and fortifications, when our miniature Admiral-in-Chief came up, her air and manner betokening serious matters.

" Peggy," said she, " in a few minutes we shall be off for Morocco."

" I hope we shan't be bound there," says the young lady, under her breath, to her other companion.

" You *are* bound there," is the natural reply.

" What are you two whispering about ? But I wish to say something to you, and you must pay attention, you American girl," that small mite goes on, undaunted. " I wish to say this. We are now leaving England on a long voyage. You must not pretend to forget that your husband distinctly placed you under my charge when he went to India, and gave me authority over you. And it is my duty to see that you behave yourself, and show yourself worthy of the name you bear and of the country you have adopted. And, mind you, I know what a grass-widow is. I know why she is called a grass-widow: it is because she is a creature that goes about gobbling up all green things—especially young men. Now, there is to be nothing of the kind on this ship. I will not have it. I am responsible for you. And look at the risk I run. Listen to this notice." She opened a paper she held in her hand, and proceeded: "' Any passenger who may take on board any article of explosive, inflammable, dangerous, or damaging nature, is liable to prosecution and to the penalties imposed by Statute, and also for all damages resulting from the shipment of such articles.' Clearly that clause refers to you; and yet here are we rendering ourselves liable unless you will pledge yourself to good behaviour."

"Aren't you going to say something for me?" murmurs Peggy, aside. "I always stick up for you when I get a chance."

To which this is the answer :—

"I have already and frequently pointed out to you that there are only two absolutely perfect human beings in the world. Now, perfection provokes envy. And envy is the mother of suspicion and malice. But when these two beings, mutually rejoicing in the consciousness of their exalted innocence, and strong in the bonds of an understanding and a sympathy that time, and fate, and traitorous tongues seem unable to destroy——"

"And particularly in this case," says Peggy, with a deeply-injured air, "when my sister Emily is going to join us at Palermo! Oh, much fun I shall have after Emily has come on board! You have never seen my sister; you don't know. I tell you we shall all have to live up to very solemn and lofty ideals when she comes along. You needn't be afraid, Missis. There won't be any skylarking, either with young men or old. Why, I used to be mortally afraid of her when she came home from school. I knew I was a frivolous person ; but I did what I could to earn her approval —at least, by concealing things—a little hypocrisy—oh, Emily believes in me—— "

"Very well, then," says Mrs. Threepenny-bit, apparently only half convinced by these protestations. "We shall see. I will keep an eye on you, my super-innocent young friend. I've seen grass-widows before, and their ways, especially on moonlight nights in the Mediterranean—— "

But here the Microscopic Calumniator had to cease, for the men were about to haul up the accommodation-ladder, and she found it necessary to move further aft.

This was a Sunday ; so that our amusements and occupations were of a subdued and sober

character.   It was not until the following day,
when we were well into the Bay of Biscay,
that we all of us seemed to settle down into
the ordinary swing of life on board ship.
And it must be said that the dreaded Bay
treated our apprehensive women-folk in the
civillest fashion.   All day long there were only
these familiar features : a cloudless sky, a
horizon of milky white, a circle of lapping,
dark-blue water, with a blinding, bewildering
shiver of diamonds towards the sun.   In the
afternoon, amid the other games going forward,
cricket was proposed ; and when the netting
had been fixed up all round, and sides chosen,
there speedily came together a little crowd of
fair spectators, who, perched high on one of
the after skylights, and forming a gallery, as
it were, could award applause or laughter as
the case demanded.   You may be sure that
Peggy was in that group, a conspicuous figure.
And one marked and beautiful thing was this :
under the widespread awning she was of course

in shadow, so that all the light that shone on her features was reflected upward from the flashing and glancing sea, and that made a sort of glory of her face. When one looked at her—at the braided golden-brown hair, the wholesome, countrified complexion, the shining eyes, the smiling mouth, the bland and yet quick interest of her expression—what did one care about this mad game except to see whether she laughed or clapped her hands in approval? These poor flannelled wretches toiling in the hot afternoon sun—with their 'Played, sir!' 'Well caught!' 'How's that?' —they were doing their best, no doubt; and the scrimmage had its varying fortunes; but here, overlooking all, was this radiant creature, complaisant, serene, beatific, the Queen of the Tournament. And already she seemed to have made friends with everybody round about her.

After dinner that night an impromptu dance was got up, when the deck-chairs had been cleared away. It was somehow a strange kind of spectacle; and yet picturesque in its bizarre fashion: the dull glow of the lamps around the red-jacketed bandsmen — the electric globes further aft revealing the awning overhead—the swift-revolving figures, the young women in light silks and cashmeres, here and there an officer in uniform—and then beyond all that the great world of waves, blue-black, smooth-heaving, with the broad pathway of the moon trembling in vivid silver. This also was curious: in an ordinary ball-room, when there is a pause in the music—a dotted note, for example, in a waltz—that momentary space of quiet is filled with the rustle of silk and muslin and slippers; but here, in these slight intervals, one caught another sound—the continuous swish of the water along the side of the ship. Wolfenberg was standing with us, looking on in his usual preoccupied, contemplative fashion.

"Isn't it very monstrous and abominable,"

said Mrs. Threepenny-bit to him, " that those
people should destroy such a beautiful night
with their scamperings?   But, after all, there
were wild revels in ' a wood near Athens.'
And it is rather pretty, don't you think so?—
the different lights—the figures—the sea :
what do you say, Mr. Wolfenberg, could an
Impressionist make something out of it ?"

" Oh, there is a subject in it," he answered
her, " for any one audacious enough.   I could
not manage it.   But Miss Dumaresq might."

She was startled, and no wonder, to hear
this master of his art talk so about a girl who
had just been a pupil in the Atelier Didron.
But he proceeded—for whenever he spoke of
Amélie Dumaresq he seemed to rouse himself
from his reveries : "You must see her work.
You will be surprised, I think.   She has the
courage of a man, and the strength of a man.
It is the truth she aims at, the truth without
compromise.   You cannot understand her
until you have seen her work.   You have met

her only in frivolous moments—and no doubt she likes to be petted."

At this moment the music ceased, and the dance came to an end.

"Miss Dumaresq is in the saloon at present, writing letters," said he, with a sudden inspiration. "Suppose we go down now, and I will ask her to bring you some of her things?"

Well, we were nothing loth; for by and by the music would be resumed; and there seemed something a little too incongruous between the silences of the great deep all around us and these strains of cornet and violin and violoncello. Besides, one naturally wished to see studies that had won commendation from so high an authority. So the four of us went along and passed down the companion-way: Miss Dumaresq we found at one of the tables, while her mother was seated at no great distance, reading.

"Amélie," said he, very gently, "may I disturb you?"

"I am delighted," said she; and at once she shut her writing-desk.

"Will you do me a favour?" he asked—and the soft black eyes answered him with a glance of obvious pleasure. "I have been talking about your work, and I want to justify myself. I want you to go and bring some of your drawings to show to our friends here."

But at this she drew back, in affected alarm.

"Oh! no, no, no!" she exclaimed. "No, I cannot, Ernest—some other time, perhaps—in daylight."

"I mean only the black and white," he pleaded.

"Oh no," said she. "No—I could not—you have taken me by surprise—I am frightened."

"Come, be yourself, Amélie!" he said, with a touch of reproach in his tone, for clearly her dismay was in a large measure simulated.

But she would not yield. She obstinately

maintained that she was terrified out of her wits ; she wanted time to prepare herself for such an ordeal ; perhaps next day she would have mustered up courage.   And of course Mrs. Threepenny-bit—not minding whether this excessive shyness were genuine or not—took the girl's part, and declared that she must be left free to choose her own time, and apologized for the suggestion having been made.   But Amélie Dumaresq's eyes were fixed on Wolfenberg.

"Ah, I see I have offended you, Ernest," she said.   "Oh yes, yes, I can see—you need not protest.   What can I do ?   I know."

She went quickly to the piano, sat down, and let her fingers run through a little prelude. She turned and looked at him, and smiled. Then she began to sing—well, it could hardly be called singing, for she had next to nothing of a voice ; but she had a pretty and coquettish grace of expression.   The air was unknown to us; the words, as we afterwards learned, were a translation from the Spanish.

' *Cupid, drop, oh drop that dart !*
Do not aim it at my heart ;
For I'm but a little maid,
And of you I'm so afraid ! '

Yes, it was pretty and fascinating enough, if it was no great vocal triumph ; and at least we could hear distinctly what she had to say. So she went on—

' *I've heard how your pranks of yore*
Kept Olympus in uproar ;
And how all the goddesses
Yielded to your sweet decrees ;
Since celestials thus you sway,
Is it any wonder, pray,
That of you I'm so afraid,
I, a little mortal maid?

I'm too young, of that I'm sure,
And too simple, to endure
Your enchantments and your errors,
Your deceptions and your terrors,
Your soft languishing desires,
Your consuming passion fires.
Out of reach and sight of man
I will keep me (if I can !)
For I'm but a little maid,
And of love I'm so afraid ! '

She came away from the piano with a laugh.

"Well, Mr. Gloomy-Brows, am I forgiven?"

"Amélie," said he, quite goodnaturedly, "how long are you going to remain a child? You forget that you are a great artist."

CHAPTER II.

TWO DISCOVERIES.

AGAIN has the mother of dawn, rosy-fingered morning, aroused the sleeping world; and over there are the phantom hills of Spain—mere films along the eastern horizon. Yet of all the passengers on board this big steamer only two have so far appeared on deck; and these have perched themselves high on the wheel-box, to be out of the way of the hose. One of these is a tall American young lady; and her eyes, which at all times are eloquent and expressive enough, are at this moment full of an eager interest.

"I am so glad of the chance," she says, "for I have a tremendous secret to tell you. Oh, you would never guess—not if you were to work at it for a month. Do you know who is on board this ship? Why, the great, the immortal 'Sappho!'"

"Oh, stuff and nonsense!"

"I tell you she is," Peggy insists. "She herself revealed to me the awful mystery last night. After you left I went back to the saloon, to get a book; and she came up and introduced herself—she's only Miss Penguin in the list of passengers, you know; but we sat down and had a nice long talk, and then she told me. Believe it or not as you like, 'Sappho' is on board this steamer."

It was a startling announcement—nay, it was almost incredible. Talk of the responsibility of the ship that bore Virgil away to Athens! Here were we carrying with us the perfervid poetess, the *Æolia puella*, the modern and much-wailing Sappho, with her distractions and agonies and cries. But in the midst of one's astonishment Peggy begins to giggle.

"I think she is horribly disappointed that

no one on board has found out who she is. But how could we? I never saw a single photograph of her in any shop. And she says her *incognito* is necessary because her sympathies with the Armenians are well known, and she is afraid the Turkish authorities might make trouble—— "

" But which is she?—which one of them is it?"

" Why, you must have noticed her—the lady who goes about leading a dog."

" What!—the dowdily-dressed woman who spends the whole of the day nursing that hideous little beast?"

" Oh, for shame! Why, that is Phaon. And isn't it too cruel, too ignominious, that Phaon has to be handed over every night to the charge of the butcher? Nobody but that unfeeling, hard-hearted Purser could have made such a stipulation."

At this point Peggy suddenly alters her tone, and becomes very confidential.

" I say, do you think I might show you a little poem ?   It was entrusted to me last night, in great secrecy ; but I rather think she would like it to be discreetly shown about. You see, it is her idea of the kind of thing that poetry should aim at.   The poets of the present day, she says, have no passion——— "

" What does an elderly spinster know about passion ? "

" I'm not good at conundrums ; I merely tell you what she says.   And here are the verses—I'll chance it ; read them and give them back to me before any one comes up."

There was no difficulty about reading them ; the handwriting was punctiliously neat.

He plucked the last long golden hair
  From off his velvet coat :
' Adieu, my Ever-fairest Fair ! '
  My lean hands seized his throat !

He groaned and gurgled to the ground,
  His white lips moaned ' Farewell ! '
High Heaven heard the awful sound—
  A shudder ran through Hell !

The whinnering whirlwind flared and fleered;
  The oak trees coiled and curled;
The gasping earth-fires glimmered weird;
  Blue lightnings shook the world.

His arms were round me in a mist;
  A simoom was his breath:
A crimson stain—ah, God, I kissed
  The Panther-Kiss of Death!

" Well ? " says Peggy.

" Why, it is just splendid ! "

" Oh, that doesn't mean anything," she retorts, with impatience. " Invent a good lie for me—do ! I must say something to her."

" Tell her that it is simply impossible for you to express your admiration."

" Hm—yes—that might answer," says Peggy, doubtfully—but at this juncture our morning conference is broken in upon, for there appears on the scene a certain Mrs. Spiteful, whose small jibes and sarcasms and enigmatic references to Magna Charta Island it is unnecessary to set down here.

A shining blue day followed—a day without

incident. Next morning found us opposite
the cliffs of Cape Roca, with the ghostly hills
of Cintra rising pale and cloud-like beyond
that silver blaze of sea. And again a perfect
day; indeed, we seemed to have got all the
winds of Æolus tied up and packed securely
away in the Purser's office. But all this time
we were getting to know more and more about
our companions, and also on occasion making
one or two new acquaintances. Amongst the
latter was a delightful old gentleman,
generally spoken of as 'the Major'—a short,
plump, roseate, cheerful, smartly-dressed person of sixty-five or so, who, from an early
part of the voyage, had clearly marked out
our Peggy for his own. But the Major had
one unfortunate failing. Ordinarily the very
soul of good nature, he nevertheless was easily
put out, just for a moment, by small trifles;
and on these occasions, and no matter who
his companion might be, he was in the habit
of using very strong language, which he

fondly imagined he uttered under his breath. Now, the Major detested Phaon, and for some reason or another detested Phaon's mistress as well; and whenever the Passionate Spinster approached Peggy, while the latter and the testy old warrior were talking together, he would mutter the most frightful anathemas, and forthwith betake himself to some other part of the ship. Indeed, Peggy was forced to complain.

"You really must speak to the Major," said she. "I never heard such profanity. Tell him he may think it, but he mustn't say it. And it's all about nothing. What has poor Phaon ever done to him? Sometimes Phaon gets his leading-string round your ankles, and trips you up; but it isn't intentional. You must tell the Major he is mistaken in supposing that people cannot overhear him. Words like 'nurse' and 'jam' are perfectly innocent, of course; but I object to the words that rhyme to them. And what harm has

Sappho done to him? She never showed
him any poetry. Once, indeed, she was
repeating to us some verses from 'The Isles
of Greece,' and when she came to 'Place me
on Sunium's marbled steep,' he said, quite
aloud, 'I wish to heavens I could—and leave
you there!' So that if anybody has the right
to be offended it is she—if she heard him—
and not he."

But we did not feel called upon to remonstrate with the Major. Human beings have
their ways; and we were well content to take
him as he was.

It was on this afternoon that Ernest
Wolfenberg came to us and said if we would
walk along to the fore saloon we should have
an opportunity of looking at some of Miss
Dumaresq's work. It was an ordeal that at
least one of us would rather not have faced.
For this was not a question of a vain and
half-cracked creature submitting her spas-
modic verses for private scrutiny. Here was

a man, himself a great artist, who believed
in the woman who was his constant companion
and friend; he seemed to think far more of
her fame and future position than of anything
pertaining to himself; and there had even
been some serious discussion about the best
method of placing a number of her water-
colour drawings before the British public.
Well, as it turned out, there was no call for
any alarm. The very first glimpse we had
of the contents of the great portfolio showed
that here was virile stuff. Blunt it might be,
and uncompromising, even brutal, in its direct-
ness; but about its strength, its vividness, its
originality there could be no doubt whatever.
And Amélie Dumaresq was no longer the
petted child; she had thrown aside that
affectation; she stood before these things
silent, not breathlessly concerned about any
judgment, nor professing to be so. And
we, ignorant as we were, surely we knew
that work of this kind, however incomplete

and immature it might be in certain ways,
had not been produced without pain and
struggle and searching of heart? There was
no fear of any critic or any school of critics
visible here. She had seen certain things
with the vision of an artist; she had aimed
at them by such methods as were known to
her; and even where a false note seemed to
have been struck, that doubtless was also
intentional. For example, there was one
drawing that represented a number of fashion-
able people promenading on a lawn—some
sea-side Sunday-morning ceremony most likely:
the women in summer costumes, white, pink,
mauve, jet-black—sunshades cream-coloured,
crimson, pure scarlet—everything clear, literal,
and distinct; but not only that; where she
had come to a gown of false green against the
true green of the grass, there it was likewise.
French, no doubt, all this was; but it had
precision and individuality; and it was an
individuality without impertinence.

No, it was not she, it was he, who seemed
a trifle nervous and anxious ; and when she
had gone away with the big portfolio, and
when he returned with us to the after-part
of the deck, his eager talk was still about her
and her pictures, defending, explaining, be-
lauding, and all the while assuming, or
appearing to assume (this was the most
curious part of it) that he, the master, the
assured and accomplished artist, and she, the
audacious amateur, were on one and the same
plane.

"What, now, do you think your Academicians would say?" he went on. "Are there
very bigoted cliques among them? Would
they denounce her for realism? And yet it
seems to me that whoever sees nothing but
realism in Miss Dumaresq's work sees nothing.
There is Art—Art speaking in one of its many
tongues, and perhaps not easily to be understood by the multitude. You are not likely
to find one gifted with her perceptions aiming

at mere fidelity, or carried away by any bald
theory about truth.   She understands as well
as any one that Art is conventional, and must
be conventional.   'Art is Art because it is
not Nature.'   Whoever talked as Shakespeare's
characters talk ?   What girl ever spoke of
cutting her lover into little stars so as to make
the heavens shine ?   These men and women
in Shakespeare's plays speak as no men or
women ever spoke ; and yet they are more
human than any men or women whom we
know or are ever likely to know.   It is simply
Art talking in one of its conventional lan-
guages ; you value it because of what it brings.
Look at our dialect stories, as they are called,"
he continued, leaning back in his deck-chair
with his hands behind his head.   " No doubt
certain peculiarities of diction are faithfully
reproduced.   But what is the value of that ?
If the human nature it reveals is poor and
mean and contemptible, what is gained by
this affectation of truth ?   For 'it is not the

truth. If you were to report a man's conversation as he speaks it, you would have a
story a life-time long. It is the business of
Art to select and condense, to pick out the
salient points of character, and speech, and
circumstance ; and I don't care how conventional the language may be so long as the
human beings live and interest me. Accuracy
is the aim of pedants and fools. When I see
Rosalind come down the stage, resplendent
in her white satin and lace veil, I don't stop
to ask where she got her wedding-dress in the
middle of the Forest of Arden. And so I
hope you have not formed any prejudice
against Miss Dumaresq's work because at first
sight it appears a literal transcript. I think
the more you study it you will perceive that
it is more than that—that it is true Art—Art
making use of a series of symbols—aiming at
just and necessary compromise—and also
expressing the individuality of the artist——"

Well, it was not for us to protest or assent ;

it was for him to lay down the law, and welcome. But there was something almost pathetic in the whole situation. It was as clear as daylight that he had thought out all these things to form a defence of Amélie Dumaresq, in case any one should object to the "realism" of her work. We had made no such objection; nay, in the case of outsiders like ourselves, what was demanded of us, and freely accorded, was appreciation, not criticism; but all the same he appeared anxious to guard against what might be the conclusions of unspoken prejudice. It was a strange kind of undertaking for one in his position. For we could not but remember what his own work was. And although scarlet sunshades against a green lawn might command one's admiration for the moment, there was something other and finer than that dwelling in our memory—there was the mystic figure of the goddess, clad in vaporous veils of rain, dim, awful, and yet benignant

as a pitying mother come up from the green
deeps to comfort her son weeping apart from
his comrades by the shores of the grey sea.
And we wondered whether Amélie Dumaresq
quite knew what manner of man this was who
thus stooped from his high estate to plead for
her and defend her, even to the belittling of
his own achievements.

But in the midst of this talk, which was
sufficiently interesting to us for several reasons,
there was a sudden and fierce ringing of the
bell—the fire-alarm ! In an instant the whole
ship was in commotion. Fore and aft there
was swift but ordered movement; certain
hands sprang to the davits to stand by the
boats — others came hurrying along with
bundles of blankets — others ran to the
hydrants. In an incredibly short space of time
every man was at his post; then there was a
pause of inspection; and then, this rapid and
unforeseen piece of drill being over, the men
gradually returned to their ordinary duties.

It was altogether admirably done ; and we saw no reason to doubt that in actual case of fire this complicated manœuvre would be gone through with equal promptitude and accuracy.

That evening found us off Cape St. Vincent. There was a certain solemnity of appearance about those high and solitary cliffs that were sombrely lit up by the after-glow streaming over from the west ; and then from time to time the tall lighthouse would send forth its silent signal—a shaft of golden flame coming out of the mystic grey of the eastern sky. But at dinner there was not much solemnity. For Amélie Dumaresq had ceased to be the artist who stood serene, and simple, and self-possessed while we looked at the contents of the big portfolio ; she was again the spoiled and petted child ; she was teasing this one and laughing towards that ; an atmosphere of enjoyment, of merriment, of delight in the mere fact of living, seemed to surround her ; while one could hardly avoid the suspicion that she was well aware of the notice she was attracting—of the covert glances that admired, or envied her, the soft clear pallor of her complexion, her long-lashed dark eyes, her cherry-red mouth, her heavily-massed black hair, with its solitary diamond star. Poor Wolfenberg was entirely neglected. It was the women she was determined to fascinate. And so, while she bedazzled them with her laughing black eyes, or charmed them with her pretty and wilful ways, or shocked them with her iconoclastic paradoxes, he was fain to turn to the only other serious person at table, and to beg for some information about the accord granted to strangers by the Royal Academy. For even while she ignored him, he remained solicitous about her interests. It was with regard to the water-colour room at Burlington House he now wanted to know.

But, as it chanced, we were on this evening to learn something more, and something surprising enough, concerning these two. For a considerable time we had lost sight of Lady Cameron, and vaguely supposed she was writing letters in the saloon, hoping to post them at Tangier. But when she did rejoin us, she had a very different tale to tell. She crept down into our snug little corner aft of the wheel-box, and began to speak in a hushed and rather eager voice; and it soon became apparent that this was no mere discovery of a sham Sappho that she had now to communicate.

"I have had a long talk with Miss Dumaresq," she said, "and I cannot tell you how she startled me. It is the saddest story —one part of it; and then the other part of it very beautiful, I think. And I was quite surprised by her manner while she was telling it. There wasn't a trace of those airs and graces; she spoke with great feeling; I could hardly have imagined her showing such sympathy——"

"Yes, but what is it all about, Peggy?"

put in Mrs. Threepenny-bit, to check this incoherent utterance.

"You will be quite as much astonished as I was," was the rejoinder, in those low and hurried tones. "And yet there is no secret about it. It is simply that _Mr. Wolfenberg is already married ——"

"Married!" said Mrs. Threepenny-bit, in dismay; but it was only her own imaginings that had been at fault.

"Oh, and to a dreadful woman!" Peggy went on. "It is the most terrible story, that side of it. A man of his refined and imaginative temperament tied to a horrid creature, a coarse, vulgar, shameless—— "

"Peggy," interposed her friend, with a little coldness, "when a young lady takes a marked and exceptional interest in a married man, I wouldn't altogether trust what that young lady might say about the married man's wife."

"But listen to this—listen to facts," Peggy persisted. "Fancy a woman who doesn't drink, but who used to pretend to drink in order to shame him before his friends! Fancy a woman who, knowing he has a particularly sensitive ear, used to take pathetic airs and bang them out on the piano as waltzes and polkas, simply to drive him from his work! Fancy a woman whose extravagance is not due to any liking for luxury, but merely because she knows it is his money she is throwing away right and left! That is a nice kind of creature for a man like Wolfenberg to be tied to!"

"Well, if it be so, it is all very sad and wretched," said the smaller woman, absently. "But it is a good thing for him he has a dream-world to take refuge in."

"Wait a moment," said Peggy. "That is only half the story. Now I come to the part of it that seems to me beautiful. Only I wish I could tell it to you as Miss Dumaresq told it to me. She spoke in quite a proud way; and then again the startling things she says don't sound so startling as coming from her, for you get used to her habit of knocking over accepted beliefs and traditions as if they were ninepins. What she practically said was this : 'The wrong that one woman has done him another woman must atone for ; and I mean to try. He shall not be left quite alone. I cannot marry him, it is true ; but if he were free to-morrow morning, I would not marry him. For one thing, marriage is the great disillusioniser. If a man and a woman have a perfect regard and esteem and affection for each other, and if they wish to preserve these, then let them remain friends, firm and fast friends, and nothing more. An exalted and devoted friendship between two people of kindred tastes and sympathies, who thoroughly understand each other, who have absolute confidence in each other, and who have a constant delight in each other's society, is a far more durable and desirable thing than marriage with its hot-headed jealousies and wrangles and, after a little while, its waning fires, followed by cold indifference.' Oh, I tell you," Peggy went on, "there is no beating about the bush with Amélie Dumaresq. She says the conjugal bond is the destroyer of all true comradeship between a man and a woman. For her own part, and quite outside these present circumstances, she says she wants to remain independent, and to have her companionship sought for as a favour and yielded voluntarily, not demanded as a right. She wants to follow out her own career, and has no mind to sink into the position of a housekeeper for any one else—looking after the dinner and the nursery. She says that if you wish the desire to meet each other, the delight in each other's society, as between a man and a woman, to be prolonged indefinitely, then do not barter away freedom and bring in the marriage pledge. Well, that is merely as regards her own position. But, really, when

she began to describe Wolfenberg's broken
life, his banishment from his own country,
his loneliness, the very piteousness of the
gratitude he shows her for her romantic
association with him, she gave evidence of
a sympathy I should not have expected of
her. To tell you the truth, I thought she was
nothing but a pert, conceited, little chatterbox,
fond of saying alarming things simply to
attract attention. But she is more than that,
Missis. I wish you heard her talk of Wolfenberg—of his simplicity of character, his
unselfishness, his sensitive honour, his noble
humility, his freedom from anything in the
shape of envy, his generous recognition of
work far inferior to his own, and I don't
know what besides. Yes, I think there is
something fine in her determination to stand
by this man, who otherwise seems so solitary.
I did not think the little Georgian, or
Virginian, or whatever she is, was capable of
rising to such a situation."

It was getting late ; the two women had to go. But already it had become abundantly clear that they regarded this discovery from very different points of view.

" It seems to me quite a beautiful relationship," said Peggy, with a touch of enthusiasm, as they were bidding each other good-night.

But the elder woman shook her head, rather sadly.

"Do you think so ? " she said. " Well, I hope it may prove to be so. But I am afraid. And wouldn't it be a terrible thing, Peggy, if the second part of your story were to turn out even more tragic than the first ?"

CHAPTER III.

A DEVIATION.

AND again comes another resplendent morning; but now we find that a brisk breeze has sprung up; the rolling and heaving blue-black waves are flashing silver crests to the sun; and far away beyond the restless plain rise the pale hills of Africa, terminating in the lofty and precipitous Cape Spartel. The two early risers are on deck, and alone.

"Listen to me," says Peggy, perching herself high and comfortably on the wheel-box—so high indeed that the light reflected upward from the sea removes the ordinary shadows from her face, and you would think there was a supernatural radiance shining there. "Do you know what the man said

after he had read aloud the Ten Commandments ? "

" There never was any such man ! " one
answers her, impatiently ; for Peggy's ways
are known.

" He said : ' And now to turn to something
really serious.' And so I want you to tell me
honestly—as honestly as you can—whether
it is true we are not going in to Tangier
after all ? "

" Well, the officers seem to say this is a
bad wind for landing ; there will be a heavy
surf."   ·ı

" Where are we going, then ? "

" Who knows ? We may turn in to Gib.
Or make for Algiers ; or Tunis. We have
no cargo to deliver or take up, so we have
all the world to choose from."

" And you consider that amusing ? I do
not in the least. For look here." She pro-
duces the table of conditions under which we
took our berths. " Did you notice this clause ?

—'*The ship may deviate for any purpose and to any extent.*' What do you think of that? What does that mean? Perhaps you rather like a deviating ship. I don't, I can tell you. Suppose it should deviate us against an unknown island?"

"It would please me to see you and the Major shipwrecked on a desert coast. You would make a romantic couple. At present it must be painful for you to know that there are about fifteen cameras on board, and that at any moment one of them may be snapping you from behind your back. Why, the universal amateur photographer must have as wholesome a constraint over you as your sister Emily."

"At all events," she retorts, "it is a good thing there is one person on board who treats me with respect. *He* wouldn't say spiteful things. He wouldn't be rude to a poor lone widow. He is always gallant, and courteous, and anxious to please. He fetches my chair

for me ; and sees that the cushion is right ;
and gives me a castle when I play chess with
him—he would give me a queen if I'd take it,
and be delighted to be beaten every time.
And just wait until we get into port : you'll
see who will have the prettiest bouquets of all
the women on this ship—and I know who will
bring them to her." Then of a sudden she
changes her tone. "I say—about Emily. I
suppose there's no doubt about our deviating
towards Palermo ? A fine thing it would be
if the Baby were left stranded all by herself in
a hotel !"

"Oh, we shall get to Palermo all right.
But why do you still call her the Baby ? She
must be nearly eighteen by now."

"She is eighteen ; and she is as tall as I
am ; and weighs five pounds more."

"A very promising Baby, indeed !"

And so as the morning went by we bored
our way into the Straits, against a hot east
wind and a heavily-running sea ; and passed

the yellow and grey scarred rock of Gib., with
Ceuta over there in the south ; and ploughed
onwards and onwards into the ever-widening
Mediterranean. Algiers, it was now known,
was our destination, and there was no murmur ;
some of us, indeed, would have been content
to leave land untouched for the next three
months if only the provisions were likely to
last. For the more we got to know of these
excellent Orotanians, the more we esteemed
them and their prevailing good humour and
kindness and courtesy ; and there were plenty
of amusements and occupations to pass those
long sunlit hours withal, even if we had not
had enough of other interests both within and
without our own small circle. For personal
relationships develop rapidly at sea ; and in
these combinations it seemed to us as though
every side of human nature was being dis-
played to us.

That evening Wolfenberg brought Amélie
Dumaresq along to our accustomed retreat,

with some little apology for the very welcome intrusion. It was a beautiful night: the sea had gone down considerably; there was a cloudless sky; a few pale stars were visible, with one golden planet shining full and clear in the deep violet vault.

"I want Miss Dumaresq to hear for herself," said he, as we made room for them, "what you think about her first coming before the British public—the best way, I mean. You say the water-colour room at the Academy is not much frequented?"

"On the contrary, it is exceedingly popular—as a rendezvous for people going to lunch."

"You would prefer a room in Bond Street— a little exhibition all to herself?" he continued. "I was only a short time in London, and got to know very few people—I was too busy with the picture-galleries; but if this project came off, I could have plenty of introductions from the other side, and we might secure two or three influential people who would get the little collection talked of. The Academicians wouldn't frown, would they, at this apparent independence?"

"Of course not. They would be more likely to come to the Private View, if you asked them."

"Not that I would have her neglect the Academy—not at all," said he, with some solicitude. "The fact is, although she has been working in oils, she is not quite so familiar with that medium yet; but later on I would have her send in a picture in oils to the Academy."

"Lady Cameron," said Miss Dumaresq, with a rueful little smile, "how would you like to be in my position? How would you like to know yourself a very small person, and find an artist like Mr. Wolfenberg bothering about you, and treating you as if you were of importance? Talk of my appealing to the British public!" she went on in another strain. "I

know who ought to appeal, and who would
appeal with some effect, and that is Mr.
Wolfenberg himself. I think it is a shame he
should be known in England only by his
reputation. But buyers are so selfish. If they
weren't so selfish I tell you what I should like.
I should like a loan exhibition in our own
country of all Mr. Wolfenberg's paintings—a
complete collection. For people are so apt to
forget what a range of subjects a painter may
have covered, and they judge him by the
picture of the moment——"

"There I don't agree with you, Amélie,"
he said, with gentleness. "The critics may.
But the public are more generous. The public
judge of a man by his best work, and give
him his reputation from his best work. When
an artist has painted a great picture, the
public give him his position; they put him
on a pedestal; and they don't call on him
to come down if his subsequent work, however
sincere, should be unequal. The world does

not bother about striking averages; that is left to the critic. The world marks the highest rung of the ladder a man has reached, and writes his name on the wall there, to remain."

"Well, Ernest, you, at least, have no right to complain of the critics; they have always been most kind to you," Miss Dumaresq interposed, pleasantly.

"The critic," he said, in an absent kind of way, "so seldom remembers that it may be himself—his own capacity or incapacity—he is revealing to the public. When Carlyle wrote his article on Scott, he was not giving us the measure of Walter Scott, he was giving us the measure of Thomas Carlyle."

But there was no indifferentism, either of manner or speech, about him when—Mrs. Dumaresq having come to call her daughter away for some purpose or another—he was left free to speak on a subject that more nearly concerned him.

"I confess," he said, "I am looking forward with a little disquiet to this visit of Miss Dumaresq's to the East. It was I who urged her mother and herself to go. I thought it would be a kind of education for Amélie; and with the future she has before her, all the best possible influences should be brought to bear on her. And yet I don't quite know that she will understand the 'brooding East'— the Mother of Dreams and Mysteries. Amélie comes of the 'impious younger world.' You must have noticed what a terribly candid mind she has," he said, rather addressing himself to Mrs. Threepenny-bit.

" Yes, indeed," said that person, frankly.

"But not hard and literal—not unreceptive," he interposed, hastily. " She has really a fine sympathy for fine things; only, as I say, the things must be fine. And she has the most profound contempt for the ordinary funny American; you need fear nothing on that score I think you said you would allow

her to go about with you a little when you
went ashore anywhere?—you see, her mother
is something of an invalid, and is not likely
to leave the ship much. And you need not
be afraid of any of that affected irreverence
—any of that continuous and feeble flippancy
that becomes so distressing."

" Oh no, no, no, Mr. Wolfenberg!" the
small woman says. " We shall be delighted
to have Miss Dumaresq with us. If we have
to fear any irreverence or mischief-making,
it is from this American-Highlander here."

" Oh, listen to her!" exclaims Peggy, with
awe-stricken eyes. " Me? You accuse me
of such a thing! And you," she goes on,
turning to her other neighbour, "what have
you to say to such a charge? Have you not
a word in my defence?"

" ' The noblest answer unto such Is perfect
stillness when they brawl.'"

But yet again Peggy speaks up on her own
behalf—and speaks up boldly too.

"Why, as for that," she says, "don't you imagine you are going to turn me into a regulation tourist. I will not be instructed on any pretence whatever. I will not follow a guide about. I will not read up history."

"Not a little English history?" puts in the small woman, with her usual ignoble sarcasm.

"And I like the notion," continues Peggy, "of you two talking to me about my serious duties!—you two, who are the most obstinately indolent, the very worst sight-seers I ever beheld! But do as you please. Swallow all the churches and mosques if you like. But not for me, thank you. Why, the only idea of an Englishman that exists in the French imagination is that he is a tall man with a red book. Well, I don't wish to be ticketed off in that way. I am a free-born American, I am. Sacramento was my dwelling-place, and Scotland is my nation——"

"What your salvation is likely to be,"

says Mrs. Threepenny-bit (for she, too, has heard of the old rhyme), " it would be hard to say—unless you keep a more civil tongue in your head."

Next morning we were nearing the end of the first stage of our voyage. And yet it cannot be said that these familiar features around us had grown in any way monotonous; nay, they had been constantly beautiful— the long decks ablaze in the sunshine; the gently-moving shadows of the ropes and spars; the soft twilight under the awnings; outside the great circle of blue sea—that deep, opaque, fierce Mediterranean blue that is like nothing else in heaven or earth; and overhead the pale sky of the south—a faint rose-purple, fading to white at the horizon. But all the same, as we slowly streamed into the vivid green waters of the harbour of Algiers, there was something in change; and the eye rather welcomed those brilliantly-coloured boats, with their swarthy boatmen.

And then, instead of sea and sky meeting featureless all around the horizon, here was a great shining city—a perfect blaze of yellow-white buildings on the face of a long ridge of hill that was crowned by far-extending masses of olive-green foliage. Picturesque enough in its way: the shimmering, translucent water, with its parti-coloured craft; then the long extent of arched stores and wharves; then the tall, French-looking terraces; then the mass of flat-roofed Moorish houses, with here and there the rounded dome of a mosque. Not so impressive, naturally, as a wholly Eastern city; but nevertheless something novel to look upon—after those long days of blue-and-silver glancing seas.

Of course there was some little excitement about going ashore : parties being hastily formed, and the eager ones getting early away in the ship's boats. Our own little group, including Wolfenberg and Miss Dumaresq, lingered for long irresolute, hardly knowing

whether it was worth while in view of our
leaving again in the afternoon ; but finally we
decided upon going in the very last boat,
which happened to be the steam-launch. And
yet it was not we who were responsible for
any delay ; it was the Passionate Poetess ; for
just as we had all got comfortably settled in
the launch, and the engineer was about to set
the screw revolving, she appealed to the
Purser.

"One moment, Mr. Purser, please ! I
really cannot leave my little dog ! I am so
afraid of those men ! I will not detain you
a minute."

Black grew the Purser's brows ; but he did
not utter a word ; while Sappho hurriedly got
out, and began to ascend the accommodation-
ladder with such speed as was possible in the
circumstances. To us it mattered little, but
she certainly was a long time away ; then we
beheld her coming down again, her precious
charge borne in one arm. Would that that

had been all! But at the foot of the ladder a dreadful accident occurred. Her foot slipped somehow; she clung to the iron stanchion with one hand; inevitably she swung round; and alas! in saving herself from being pitched headforemost into the sea, she was forced for a moment to abandon Phaon, who incontinently tumbled down on to the grating and next into the water. Immediately there was a mighty commotion: it was as if a baby had to be saved. Arms were stretched out—and stretched out in vain; Sappho, who had sprung on board the launch, called frantically on Phaon; while the fat little grey pug, with his black snout and wrinkled forehead well out of water, was splashing away with his fore-paws, and swimming, as much as he could swim, in the wrong direction. And then the man at the bow, seizing a boat-hook, made a dash at him. Sappho shrieked.

"Don't!—don't!—you'll kill him!" she called, piteously; for she evidently thought the man wanted to gaff the animal, as one would gaff a salmon.

But what he really meant to do was to hook up the silken string attached to Phaon's collar; and in this he succeeded; the dog was led down aft, and hauled on board, and delivered to his mistress; and she, exhausted by these wild emotions, and overjoyed to get her beloved into the very midst of us, made him finally secure by depositing him, stream-ing, and shaking himself, and winking his beady eyes, right on to the Major's polished boots.

What our respected friend said upon this occasion can never now be known; for there was a sudden rattle of the engine, and a whirr of the screw; but, as he tried to withdraw his feet from under this sprawling encumbrance, there was a look on his face that was too awful to contemplate without apprehension. And what must she do but heap insult upon injury?

" Major, would you mind holding this for

a moment?" she said, handing him the blue silken string. "Phaon is so impulsive—so impetuous—— "

"Nurse and jam the confounded little beast!" said the Major—or rather it was something resembling these sounds that escaped from between his set teeth; but probably she did not hear, for there was such a spluttering noise from the engine. At all events, he was forced to hold the string for her; while she proceeded to open her hand-bag, and from thence she took a small brush, and with that she began to smooth down Phaon's dripping coat, while in vain did the Major try to get his feet away from the prancing and dancing of those four restless legs. We began to fear that Phaon would not see the end of this voyage.

Meanwhile we got ashore, and climbed the stifling hot steps, and crossed the blinding white Boulevard, and were glad to escape from the glare of the sunlight into the cool

shadows of the Jardin Marengo, with its
branching palms, and bamboos, and tall
tamarinds. But Mrs. Threepenny-bit, mind-
ful of former days on the Nile, and anxious
to renew her acquaintance with those Arabs
whose dignity of deportment she had always
so much admired, was soon ready to be off
again. Had she not under her wing this
young American, whose nascent artist-mind
was hungering after new impressions ?

And as we went wandering idly through
the town, choosing the more shaded thoroughfares, one could not but admire the delicate
way in which Wolfenberg recognized that
Amélie Dumaresq had been confided to the
elder lady's charge. He claimed no right of
association ; he was just as the others ; nay,
he rather kept away from her. But at times,
of course, he had to call her attention to this
thing or that ; and then he would do so in a
curiously respectful way. For example, in the
Rue Bab Azoun we came upon an oddly

incongruous sight—a shabby-looking little French omnibus filled with grave and stately and silent Arabs, in their turbans and flowing white robes.

"Amélie," he said, stepping up to her, "there is a subject for you."

She glanced in the direction indicated.

"It is too bizarre," she answered him.

"It is Algiers," he said, and then he fell back again into the order of our procession.

For we were going two and two, and even then we did not escape remark. The Major and Lady Cameron led the way; and no doubt they were conspicuously foreigners; the Major being plump, and fresh-coloured, and cheerful-looking, while Peggy was tall, and fair-complexioned, and handsome. And now it was that Mrs. Threepenny-bit grew wroth. For while the Arabs, calm, serious, impassive of demeanour, went by without appearing to take the slightest notice of us, the low-class French population turned to stare at the strangers, grinning, chattering, and nudging each other. Nay, one yellow-skinned little wretch of a boy had the audacity to look up at our Peggy, and say "Ole raight!" This it was that set the smaller woman's soul ablaze.

"Miss Dumaresq," said she, "has it ever occurred to you that it is only the northern nations of Europe that have the faculty of laughing? The French never laugh. They haven't the physique. They can only snigger." Here, indeed, was a stupendous generalization; and all because an impudent little Algerian gamin had mocked at our tall young friend from Inverfask.

There was, of course, nothing of this kind when we had got away up into the Arab quarter of the city. As we were slowly perambulating the steep and narrow thoroughfares, and admiring the endless variety and picturesqueness of costume and colour, Miss Dumaresq turned to her temporary guardian.

"When we came ashore at first," said she, "I

thought we had made a mistake. I thought we had got into nothing but a second-rate French town. But now I should like to spend six months in Algiers—or three or four times that."

"You are beginning too soon," said her companion, with a smile. "At least, if you go on in the same way, by the time we have finished this voyage you will have formed plans for two lifetimes."

When at last we made away back again for the Boulevard, and came in sight of the Hôtel de l'Europe, we descried various groups of our fellow-Orotanians, just as you are sure to find English people hanging about Shepheard's Hotel in Cairo. The first person we encountered inside was the Passionate Spinster, who was in dire distress, for she could get nobody to attend to her. So she threw herself upon us. She besought the Major to find a safe corner in the saloon, where Phaon might be tied up. She asked if she might have a seat at our table. And when, after lunch, it was suggested that, instead of sending for two carriages, we ought simply to charter one of those small omnibuses with the open windows and curtains, which would be so much cooler, and would accommodate the whole of us, she eagerly embraced that proposition, counting herself in. And thus it was that she who claimed kinship with 'the Lesbian woman of immortal fame' bestowed her society on us during our drive out to Mustafa Inférieur. Why not? After all, human beings are of different kinds, and the world is wide.

"Yes, but an Algerian omnibus is narrow," said the Major, subsequently; and the mere recollection of his sufferings once more aroused in him a furious wrath. "By heavens, I will strangle that little beast if it ever comes near my legs or feet again!"

Before we got under weigh that afternoon an apparently trifling incident occurred which we had occasion afterwards to recall. A

French Colonel and his wife, with their little
girl, had come out to look over the ship; and
while the former were talking to the captain,
the latter was being made much of by a
number of the young ladies on board. But
this small creature of seven or eight remained
proof against all their blandishments. She
was absolutely imperturbable, regarding them,
it is true, but not responding in any way
whatever. They tried her with various kinds
of French, including that of Ollendorff and
that of Stratford-atte-Bowe—*Aimez-vous
l'Afrique?* . . . *Vas-tu promener partout
à voir le vaisseau?* . . . *Allons, descendons
au salon et je te donnerai des sucrés.* . . .
Petite, serrez les mains chez moi. . . .
Travaillez-vous à vos leçons, mademoiselle?
. . . *N'avez vous pas une seule parole pour
nous?* . . . *As-tu regardé le capitaine de la
shippe?* . . . Such were the rags and tags of
this ingenuous and one-sided conversation that
came floating towards us. But no; they could

win no response. She remained quite impassive and silent.

Now it was at this moment that a young
Russian who had not gone ashore—indeed, he
had hitherto mixed but little with his fellow-
passengers—came along, took up the book he
had left in his deck-chair, and, sitting down,
began to read. He was quite near to this
small child, but he did not pay any attention
to her; she, on the contrary, regarded him
attentively for a moment or two, and then,
as if drawn by curiosity or by some more
occult attraction, went close up to his chair.
He became aware of her approach, and raised
his eyes from his book. Very beautiful eyes
they were, if it is not absurd to call a man's
eyes beautiful—blue-grey, dark-lashed, and
full of light; and when they were bent on this
small, inquisitive stranger, she, who had hitherto seemed so entirely abstracted and indifferent,
smiled in response. Nay, she held out her
tiny hand. "Bonjour, monsieur!" she said.

And of course he accepted that timid proffer
of comradeship at once ; he spoke to her ; she
replied to him, in her pretty and childish way ;
and so, in the most simple and easy fashion in
the world, these two had become friends.

"Did you notice that ?—isn't that remarkable ?" said Amélie Dumaresq, in a quick
undertone, to Wolfenberg. "Tell me, Ernest,
who is he ?—he hardly ever speaks to any one."

"He is a Russian—Hitrovo—Paul Hitrovo,"
was the answer, also uttered guardedly.

"Do you know him ? Have you talked
with him ?"

"A little."

"Will you introduce him to me—some
other time ? "

Wolfenberg looked surprised, almost startled.

"Oh yes, if you wish it—oh yes, certainly,"
he said—while the fascinated small French
girl was still standing by Paul Hitrovo's chair,
listening to him, and looking up into his
smiling eyes.

CHAPTER IV.

AN INTRODUCTION.

AND again the gods have given us a gracious morning; the heavens cloudless and serene; the far-stretching circle of the sea rolling its blue-black waves and lapping and flashing in the sun; an unstable world save for the long and mountainous rampart down there in the south—the grey-scarred and sterile-looking cliffs of the African coast. And here, under the welcome shade of the awning, one comes upon two of the passengers who appear to be in close and earnest confabulation. It is of Wolfenberg and Amélie Dumaresq they are talking.

"Well, Missis," says the Lady of Inverfask, addressing her friend by the last invented of all her innumerable sobriquets, "I cannot understand why you should be so apprehensive. You yourself admit that such a relationship would be beautiful, if only it could be made permanent. What is to hinder its being permanent? Miss Dumaresq would tell you that it is all the more likely to last because there is no bond, because it is voluntary, because each knows that the other could break away. What she says is simply this: 'Husbands and wives lead a far happier life, a far more equable and contented life, when they have ceased to be lovers, and have become good friends. Why, then, should not Mr. Wolfenberg and I take up the latter half of this relationship, since the former is impossible?' You know her frank way of speaking. And her ideas are as clear as her speech. She is no school-girl, with her head full of sentiment and dreams. She has seen the world. She has had experience of men—and not a very fortunate one, I imagine: you see

the family are rich; and I rather fancy, from
one or two things she said, that she has made
unpleasant discoveries—or, at least, had unpleasant suspicions—with regard to certain of
the young men who came about her. But
here is a man whom she can absolutely trust;
whom she admires and respects beyond
measure; with whom she is in sympathy on
every point; and why should not their close
and constant association together be as
permanent as any marriage-bond? According
to her, it is the conjugal relationship that dis-
enchants; here there can be no disenchantment;
they remain to each other just as they are.
And look at their comradeship in art: another
tie. She must perceive that he has all the
qualities that she lacks: another reason for
sympathy. And then his solitary position;
she pities him; she is resolved to stand by
him—oh, I don't see that you should be so
apprehensive!"

For a second or two the smaller woman was

silent—looking absently across the flashing
waters to the pale line of mountainous coast.
At last she said—

"Well, Peggy, if I were Mr. Wolfenberg, I
would go ashore at the very first port we come
to, and I would make my way back to
America."

"To be met at New York by that woman,
with a troop of her drunken companions?"

The conversation could not be continued
further; for at this moment Miss Dumaresq
herself appeared, coming quickly along the
deck, her head raised and careless, her arms
swinging a little with the mere exuberance of
life. The small and graceful figure looked neat
in its Sunday-morning costume of black silk
and white frills; and when she came up it was
apparent that she had paid particular heed to
her toilet—the high-arched, dark eyebrows had
been touched, perhaps also the pretty mouth.
But it was not of that she was thinking.

"I have some news for you," said she, with

great animation, and her brilliant black eyes were full of pleasure and eagerness, "but it must not be spoken of; you must not mention it to any one; and especially not to Mr. Wolfenberg. He has just been telling me; and what a surprise it is! For we quite understood that he was going to take the full seven weeks' holiday; but with an artist like him a sudden inspiration takes possession; and it is no use his trying to put it aside and turn to it later on. What do you think, then, of the subject Mr. Wolfenberg is considering? —the Fountain of Callirrhoe!" She was quite breathless with the joy of this discovery; but she had to speak in tones of subdued excitement, for there were other people now coming along. "Can you not imagine what he will make of it—the deserted Greek girl killing herself by the side of the water—or, perhaps, the dead girl disappearing—I don't know, but this I do know, that it will be something to make one's fingers tremble and make one's eyes fill. It will be splendid — splendid! And no one must speak to him about it, or he will be anxious and discontented, and perhaps throw the subject aside altogether; no, it must be allowed to grow up of itself in his mind, quite in silence, and then—then some day you will see! And just think of this: he has asked my advice!—*my* advice!—as if I and my wooden dolls could be of any use to him! Prospero, the master of spirits, come to ask the advice of Caliban carving sticks!"

"At least it was a great honour," said Peggy.

"And now he will dream about that all the way until we get to Athens," she went on— and really this exhilaration of interest added quite a new charm to the pretty face and the lustrous dark eyes; "and it does not matter whether the real fountain, if there is one, lends itself well or not: the picture will be already complete in his mind. I am delighted! You know I was rather afraid that mother and I had forced this idleness on him—he is so ready to sacrifice himself; and I feared, too, he might be bored by the society of two women. But now I am quite at ease. Now he will never want for companionship and for occupation so long as he has his picture to think about; and when you notice him walking up and down by himself, and not speaking to any one, you need not imagine he is idle. Ah, I tell you, you will see something when you see the Fountain of Callirrhoe!"

Welcome news; but perhaps we were even better pleased, and more interested, in observing the genuine enthusiasm with which this girl spoke of Wolfenberg's work. That was at least one bond the more between these two oddly situated persons.

This was a Sunday morning; there was service on deck, under the awning; the young women's voices sounded sweet and clear above the monotonous swish of the waves along the vessel's side.

In the afternoon the Passionate Spinster
bore down upon us, bringing with her a whole
armful of translations—and Lempriere. There
was no escape; she had skilfully cut off
retreat; and soon the tale of her unnumbered
woes was unfolded. It turned out that she
had heard from one of the officers that on the
following morning we should be within sight
of the shores of Sicily, the song-haunted
island; and with a generous ardour she had
set to work to prepare herself, first of all by
tracing out the wanderings of Ulysses. But
there were riddles and disappointments in the
way; and now, as she spoke, the sandy-haired
woman with the cold grey eyes seemed to be
in a bit of a temper.

"It really is too bad!" she said, fretfully.
"You can't trust one of these books. You
would think that since they have been labouring away at their mechanical tasks through
so many generations, there might be a little
agreement among them. But why does one

say, 'mother of dawn, the rosy-fingered morning,' while another says, 'daughter of dawn, the rosy-fingered morning;' and why do they write Aias when they mean Ajax; and what on earth is the use of saying Peleides instead of Achilles, and Atreides instead of Agamemnon?"

Now these were amazing questions to come from the perfervid Sappho, who continually adorns her pages with copious quotations from the Greek and Latin—inaccurate for the most part, no doubt, but of excellent intention.

"However, it is the geography that is most irritating," she continues, with more than a "snap" of anger in her voice. "Look at the confusion caused by having Phæacia, Scheria, Corcyra, Corfu—four names—all for the same place! And one writer tells you that Calypso's island is Gozo, which is close by Malta, and another declares that it is Ogygia, supposed to be opposite Lacinium!"

At this point, unhappily, the volume of

Lempriere fell upon Phaon; and the lamentable howl that the poor little beast set up awoke the Major, who was asleep in a neighbouring chair. The Major turned round, glared, muttered something, doubtless of an unholy character, to himself—and then, struggling to his feet, made his way to the grating surrounding the wheel-box, where he again sought soft slumber, though in a far more uncomfortable position.

"You see they *will not* call anything by a simple name!" exclaimed our poetess, with a savage wrath which we were sorry to see agitating so celestial a mind. "When Ulysses, after leaving Æolia, is ship-wrecked, he is thrown upon the coasts of the Læstrygones; but the coasts of the Læstrygones are simply Sicily!—and it is Sicily that he has quite recently left, after having escaped from the giant Polyphemus——"

"Miss Penguin, why should you bother with boys' stories!" interposed Amélie

Dumaresq, with a touch of disdain. "Sicily
for me will be the land of Hermione, and
Perdita, and the good Camillo, and the statue
that becomes a woman before the eyes of the
King. That is something worth thinking
about!"

"And I," puts in our Peggy, "am going
to find out from which port Antigonus and
Hermione's child could have sailed when they
were blown on the shores of Bohemia."

"The shores of Bohemia?" is the in-
credulous cry.

"Yes," she says, calmly. "Didn't you
know that the dukes of Bohemia had
possessions and seaports on the Adriatic
coast?" For Peggy is always flourishing
this profound piece of erudition before us—
though some of us may have dark doubts as
to its authenticity.

Meanwhile, what had become of the young
Russian whose beautiful eyes had thawed the
frigidity of the little French girl; and what

had become of the introduction that Amélie Dumaresq had asked for? Well, for one thing, M. Paul Hitrovo was rather a mysterious and enigmatical young man. Beyond the fact that he generally passed the morning in the deck smoking-room, whiling away the time with cigarettes, no one could say precisely how or where he spent the remainder of the day. He rarely mixed with his fellow-passengers; he never joined in any of the games going forward; he came late to meals, and remained after the others had left. Then, again, a formal introduction is an unusual, and a marked, thing on board ship: we could understand Wolfenberg's embarrassment over her blunt request. On board ship people make each other's acquaintance through a variety of little accidents, or through some chance talking to a common friend. But as for going to a young man and saying that a certain young lady wished that he should be introduced to her—how was such a thing to be done, especially when the go-between was so proud and sensitive a person as Ernest Wolfenberg? He of all men would be the first to shrink from anything that seemed to compromise, in the remotest degree, this young lady who had made so unexpected a demand.

And, indeed, it was in an entirely haphazard fashion that their coming together was accomplished, on this same Sunday afternoon. The Dumaresqs and several others had gone below to have tea, and they had just taken their places when Hitrovo came into the saloon, looking around him in his customary indolent, good-natured way.

"Won't you come to our table?" said Wolfenberg.

"If I may," he answered, smiling; and forthwith he installed himself in one of the chairs, opposite Miss Dumaresq and her mother.

There was no set introduction. After a

second or two he quite naturally and simply
joined in the general talk, speaking excellent
English, with hardly a trace of accent. He
was singularly good-looking; he had pleasant
manners; so far from trying to impress or
shine, he seemed in a measure indifferent;
and those clear blue-grey eyes of his, when
they lighted on a woman, bespoke favour for
him. But the curious thing was that his
coming to this table appeared to have frozen
up Amélie Dumaresq. Ordinarily eager and
animated, thrilling with life and loquacious,
she was now constrained and embarrassed;
she did not glance his way at all; she kept
her eyes downcast or averted; she was silent.
Her mother might join in this random conversation about the ship and our prospects:
she had not one word. For the first time
since we had made her acquaintance she
seemed to have lost her self-possession; and
on that account it was all the more marked.
But Hitrovo did not appear to notice; he had

enough to do in talking to these other ladies, who were all more or less strangers to him. And when at length he went away, it was clear that he had impressed them most favourably.

"Well, Amélie, I brought him to you," Wolfenberg said, with a smile.

"Yes, Ernest," she answered, with some touch of confusion. "I—I did want to find out something about him—after the incident with the little French girl. That struck me. But I hardly wonder at it. He has extraordinary eyes."

So she had glanced at him, after all?

"That French child," said Mrs. Dumaresq, "has began early to find out that gentlemen's eyes may be attractive."

"There was more than that, mamma. She went up to him while he was still reading," the daughter made reply; but she was clearly not inclined to enter into any discussion about this young man, or his looks, or ways, or manners. Presently she rose and left the table, and went up on deck, taking her book with her, and choosing a chair where she could be by herself.

Towards evening we could make out the sharp peaks of Galita island, far away ahead of us in the mystic grey of the east; and as night closed round us there was the golden ray of the lighthouse streaming out from time to time.

The morning found us among the Ægadean Isles, off the west coast of Sicily—those lonely and voiceless rocks, lofty, and arid, and scarred —their ruddy cliffs set in a perfect calm of blue sea. Sappho was running all about the ship imploring people to tell her whether it was on the mainland or on one of those islands that Ulysses encountered the Cyclops; Peggy was delighted to discover that we should reach Palermo early in the afternoon, for she wanted to snatch away the Baby from all possibility of brigands; Mrs. Threepenny-bit was expecting letters, to learn how many more teeth her precious boys had had knocked out at football; and the Major was secretly disclosing to one or two friends a plan he had formed for enticing Phaon away from his mistress in the streets of Palermo, and introducing him to a sausage-maker. In short, there was quite a stir with the beginning of the new week and our nearing another halting-place. Even Paul Hitrovo came on deck, and talked a little with Mrs. Dumaresq, her daughter standing by, looking on and listening.

But it was with Wolfenberg that Amélie Dumaresq spent most of the morning and noon, for no doubt the two artists had much to observe and talk of in common, as we steamed on by Cape St. Vito, and across the Gulf of Castellamare, and past the evil-named Punta dell'Uomo Morto, making onwards for Cape Gallo. This northern coast of Sicily is magnificently picturesque: vast and precipitous cliffs of a sombre red, here and there rising into darker peaks, about as sharp as the Aiguilles overlooking the Mer de Glace, here and there dipping down into a spacious valley, with groves of orange and citron sweltering in the heat. A lonely coast it seemed, too : it was at long intervals that a little grey powder, as it were—a thin, insignificant line at the foot of those giant cliffs—revealed a village down by the shore. In times of storm and louring skies, these bold headlands, and the long spurs terminating in a solitary lighthouse, must look grand indeed ; but now, as we saw them across the trembling and shimmering blue sea, they had grown visionary and spectral in the haze of settled fine weather. The intervening air seemed to be dense with sunlight.

And what did those two think of Palermo —Palermo the Superb—as we slowly steamed into the pellucid green water ? To the non-professional eye the more striking features were obvious enough : a noble bay, far extending, with long moles and promenades; white terraces just above the sea; public gardens, with foliage of freshest verdure; then the gradually-ascending town, with its countless domes and spires; and behind all that a mighty semicircle of mountains, twisted and torn and thrown about as if by the hand of some scene-painter gone out of his senses. Indeed, one began to ask one's-self if all this were quite real—if it were solid, in fact. Was there not some strange suggestion of a huge wooden frame, with a breadth of shivering canvas stretched over it? Those white terraces, and green gardens, and domes and spires, and wildly-twisted mountain-peaks : were they permeable to a draught of air coming from over the stalls? And if one were to whistle suddenly, would not a number of dusky and shabby men immediately rush out and run the whole panoramic thing away on wheels?

If this was what Amélie Dumaresq was thinking of the imposing city before her, she was speedily startled out of her reverie. All at once, and just as we were about getting to our anchorage, but while there was still considerable way on the vessel, it was discovered that the steam steering-gear had got out of order. The swiftness with which this mishap was rectified was admirable. Before any of the passengers quite understood what had happened, the first officer and four or five of the hands had hurried aft to the wheel, unshipped the case, got the mechanism into working-trim, and the next minute the ship was answering her helm just as if nothing had occurred. And presently we heard the sonorous call, "Let go the anchor!"—followed by a roar and a plunge that must have made that canvas city quake.

Then the various boats that had come out from the harbour—heavily built craft, most

of them, and gay of colour—began to make
for the steamer; while on board there was
a good deal of bustle among those preparing
to go ashore. But we were never among
the first of these; and so it chanced that
Mrs. Threepenny-bit was idly gazing over
the side, when her eye caught sight of
something.

"Peggy," she called, "here are some visitors
in one of the boats—is this your sister?"

Peggy came running.

"Oh, good gracious, it's the Baby!" she
cried, in wild delight. "And these are the
Vincents with her—how kind of them!—they
have brought her over from Naples." And
with that she waved her handkerchief frantically, and succeeded in arresting their attention, for there was an answering signal; and
then she went quickly to the top of the accommodation-ladder; and probably she would
even have descended the steps to meet them—
disarranging all the traffic—but that the third

officer, who was busily engaged in getting his boat-loads away, sternly refused to allow her. Well, not very sternly, perhaps. The fact is, it seemed to us that this young man never missed an opportunity of conversing with Peggy; and even now, while he was occupied in packing off the passengers, he found quite enough time to chat with her. No, not at all sternly; for more than one waltz had she given him on those marvellous moonlit nights off the coast of Portugal, and many another he might reasonably hope to secure before we saw English land again. In truth it was simply to talk to her that he detained her at the top of the ladder.

At last the way was clear; and here was the Baby—blushing furiously at the amount of attention bestowed on her—ascending the steps. And it was not until the two sisters had got through a considerable amount of hugging, and kissing, and laughing, and questioning, that we had a chance of seeing

what " my sister Emily " was like. She was
brought forward to us—and her friends accompanied her. Well, she was no rival to
our peerless and incomparable Peggy; that
was not to be expected; but she was a
good-looking lass none the less—ingenuous
of aspect, and grave—timid also, though that
may have been because of her suddenly
finding herself among strangers. She was
not so fair as Peggy; nor so slender either;
she promised to be of the Amazon type; but
yet there was something very winning about
her shy ways, and her self-consciousness, and
her modest desire to please. As for Peggy,
she made no concealment as to the alteration
in her own life likely to be caused by the
arrival of this serious-eyed young maid; with
a sigh of regret she relinquished her past
privileges and freedom from restraint; there
would be no more fun for her now, she said,
since the Baby had come on board.

Well, we lazy folk did not care to go ashore

this afternoon; Amélie Dumaresq had for once persuaded her mother to bestir herself; and those two and Wolfenberg — the faithful Wolfenberg—went away by themselves. The good friends with whom the Baby had been travelling were much interested in the ship; they spent a considerable time in exploring it; and in the end they were easily persuaded to stay to dinner. And on this evening it must be admitted that Palermo retrieved itself; it cast aside that look of a sad and bad and mad chromo-lithograph; it assumed dignity when the arid hills grew dark and solemn against the westering glow, and the lighthouses began to send their steady rays through the gathering dusk. Mystery—sentiment—the subtle, elusive, imaginative quality in landscape that is unapproachable by inferior or mechanical art—was now in the air, as "the sun sank, and all the ways were overshadowed." Then minute points of fire began to appear here and there in the town like golden glowworms. And these again, as the night fell, were outshone by others of a very different colour, the blue-white radiant stars of the electric lamps along the esplanade, that sent long, quivering reflections down on the smooth-heaving black water between us and the shore. Palermo was now brilliantly illuminated—a blaze of splendour; for there was a public *festa* in the gardens of the Villa Giulia, and that also helped. The whole dark surface of the sea was dancing and glittering with those will-o'-the-wisps of imaged lights.

Our new friends stayed late, chatting on deck; but when at length they decided to go, we took them along to the top of the accommodation-ladder, so that they should have the first chance of a boat returning to the shore. And just as we reached the gangway, who should appear but the Dumaresqs, mother and daughter, Amélie Dumaresq being in a very gay and laughing and vivacious mood.

But it was not Wolfenberg alone who was
their escort : the dull, orange-hued glow of
the lamp showed us that there were two
gentlemen following them upwards from that
black gulf of water.   And the fourth member
of the party turned out to be Paul Hitrovo :
we learned that he had been so kind as to
accompany the two ladies, along with Wolfenberg, to the festival in the gardens of the
Villa Giulia.

CHAPTER V.

A HOROSCOPE.

As we make for the shore on this fair-shining morning there is a heavy ground-swell running in : long, smooth, unbroken, oily-green waves that lift the steam-launch high in air and seem to leave it suspended for a time, until it glides down again, spluttering and snorting and rolling, into the next great ocean-valley. The boat is filled with our good Orotanians ; and there is quite a blaze of white costumes ; for the sun promises to be fierce. Some, whom we hardly envy, are about to ride away up to the top of Monte Pellegrino—the vast brown slope beyond the bay is already shimmering in the heat ; others, of more modest ambition, mean simply to wander about the shady

thoroughfares of the city, studying the remains
of Moorish architecture; as for our small party,
we are bent on a pious pilgrimage to the
distant Monreale among the hills.   And who
so proud as the Major on this auspicious
morning—the Major, to whom we have handed
over Lady Cameron and her sister?   For
what with the advent of the Baby, and what
with Mrs. Dumaresq having again consigned
her daughter to our care, it is obvious that
we shall have to separate into two carriages
as soon as we reach the shore; and who so
competent to take command of one of these
as our gallant if elderly soldier?   Joyful,
indeed, is the Major, and assiduous; Peggy
looks demure, taking care not to meet the
grave glances of her friends; while the Baby,
serious, unconscious, regards in an impressed
kind of way the great panoramic town and
its background of mountains.   Mrs. Threepenny-bit has declared herself quite charmed
with the Baby.   Her ingenuousness, she

affirms, is as sweet and fresh and wholesome as the flowers in a cottage garden. There are no underhand ways about *her*. *Her* eyes never say two things at once. *She* wouldn't sit in corners, and speak low, and ignore a whole room-full of people for the sake of one. And so forth. It is curious to notice how envy crops up on the most unexpected occasions.

But, as it chanced, a sad fate befell the Major after all. On landing at the mole, we found ourselves surrounded by a wildly-gesticulatory crowd of drivers and would-be guides; there was nothing for it but to push through these, unheeding, and take forcible possession of the nearest vehicle, Miss Dumaresq being pulled in by Mrs. Threepenny-bit with much adroitness. Then we turned to see how the Major and his charges were getting on. Well, he had secured a carriage; and he had got the two ladies safely deposited therein; and doubtless he was about to join them, when at this very moment the Passionate Poetess came up, carrying Phaon in her arms. The clamour of this crowd of unwashed Sicilians prevented our hearing what she said; but what took place was clear enough. Sappho was appealing to Lady Cameron to let her have the vacant seat in the carriage; and at once Peggy—who is the soul of good nature—smilingly assented; while the Baby politely changed over to the other side. Then we saw the Major compelled to assist his deadly enemy to her place, and not only that, but he had to shove Phaon along before he could himself follow. *Avanti!* And when Amélie Dumaresq's face appeared again from behind her sunshade, she was wiping away the tears from her eyes. She had been outrageously, and wickedly, and cruelly laughing.

And very merry and light-hearted was she as we drove away through the town and out into the open and ever-ascending country. Wolfenberg smiled in a calmly tolerant fashion.

###########

It was no business of his to play the part of tutor; nay, he was always glad when he saw her amused or amusing others. And yet it must be said for this young lady that, however careless she might seem of her surroundings, there was very little escaped her sharp and observant eyes. She might be laughing and telling stories of her fellow-students at the Atelier Didron; but her glance took note of one object after another—a Moorish-looking building, a gaily-decorated cart, a horse staggering along under an enormous load, and suffering from hideous sores (though nobody is likely to miss *that* familiar feature of a Sicilian highway). And at last she said:

"Ernest, when my little exhibition is opened in London, I must send an invitation to Papa Didron. Do you think he will come over? Well, I fear not; he is too busy. But he must know of my great importance."

"I will take care of that, Amélie," said Wolfenberg, who not only invariably talked as though this constant companionship between herself and him was to last through all the years of their life, but also, in this particular instance, as though he were going to act the part of showman for her. " I will make sure of that. For one thing, I must get to know the London correspondents of the Paris papers; they may be interested; they ought to notice the pictures. Why, it is a piece of news. And then you are a daughter of France as far as art is concerned."

"Oh, listen to him!" she said to Mrs. Threepenny-bit, in simulated horror.

" I don't mean as regards landscape," he interposed, good-naturedly. " I know your heretical opinion of French landscape—— "

" French landscape!" she said, in open disdain. " French landscape is landscape seen by limelight; all very effective, no doubt, in spinach green, and cold grey, and black; but where is the luminosity, where is the sunlight, where is the throbbing air? And yet how

can you wonder?" she went on, apparently
for the mere amusement of the thing—for her
vehemence seemed a little bit assumed.
" What are the poor men to do? God
made the world out of nothing; but French
artists are not quite so clever—they can't
make landscapes out of those monotonous and
treeless wastes; and so they construct effective
studies of light and shade—limelight and false
shade. And England is just as bad in the
opposite direction. England is too con-
ventionally picturesque. The mist gives you
the atmospheric values all ready-made to hand.
The clouds are low down, and come easily into
the picture; distances are arranged for you;
and then the country is all broken up with
hedges, and coppices, and small fields, and
farms—everything you could wish. Now, at
home—in America, I mean—you have to
wrestle with your subject—you have got to
face it—the light is clear and hard—there is
no compromise."

"There never is any compromise about you, Amélie," Wolfenberg said, laughing. "But if you wish to see throbbing air and luminosity, just you get up in the carriage and look back."

For by this time the patient horses had dragged us away up towards La Rocca; and when we rose to regard the landscape that now stretched out far below us, we beheld the famous Conca d'Oro, that immense and fertile valley filled with the fresh deep green of orange groves and lemon groves, with the dusty heights of Monte Grifone rising on the right, while in front, and away beyond the partly-hidden city, the vast breadth of pale blue sea trembled through the heat.

"I must get down," she said; "there is more freedom to look about when you are walking."

And indeed our slim-built and energetic Peggy had already descended from the other vehicle; and so had the Baby; and so had their gallant escort; Sappho and the pug

remaining in sole possession of the carriage.
And thus the re-united party went forward
together, leisurely climbing the white and
dusty road; our goal, the Fiesole-like Monreale, perched high on a hill, being now within
view. Hot it was. The Major began to
murmur hints about a *trattore*, and about a
bottle of something combined with seltzer.
The arid rock by the wayside had been hewn
into small terraces by the cactus-growers; and
the prickly pears had borrowed a charming
tinge of colour from the sun; but the one or
two we tried afforded us no kind of satisfaction.
The only cool thing visible was the fresh green
of the great valley: it was pleasant to let the
eyes wander down towards those far-stretching,
dense, luxuriant orange groves.

When at length we had toiled up to the
queer, deserted-looking little town, we made
straight for the Duomo, which, in truth, was
the only thing we had come to see. But on
entering the square, we perceived that we were

not the first of the Orotanians : Paul Hitrovo
and a companion, whose acquaintance he had
made on board, were standing on the pavement just outside the Cathedral, the former
smoking a cigarette.

"Well, that is a surprise!—I wonder if he
has sat up all night?" said Mrs. Threepenny-
bit, who had never been too favourably disposed
towards this young man, despite his achieve-
ment of fascinating the small Algerian.
"Major," she continued in an undertone,
"everybody gets to hear everything about
everybody else on board ship. Who *is* that
Mr. Hitrovo?"

"Gad, I don't know," said the Major, con-
tentedly. "You'd better ask the young
ladies : they seem mostly interested in him."

"The common gossip," put in Wolfenberg,
with a certain quiet indifference, "is that he
is of a very good Russian family. Lives in
Vienna, mostly ; and belongs to the sporting
circles there. He told me himself that he

had won the Prix de Consolation at Monte
Carlo last year—pigeon-shooting."

"But what could have induced him to take
a voyage like this—without knowing a single
soul on board, apparently?" she demanded
again.

"That I cannot say," he made answer.
"Sheer idleness comes as a relief sometimes—
but not often to one of his age."

As they spoke, Amélie Dumaresq had
glanced from the one to the other, quickly and
furtively; but she said no word; indeed she
could not; for now we were approaching the
great doors of the Cathedral, and here were
Hitrovo and his fellow Orotanian raising their
hats as the ladies went by. The next moment
we were in a still and hushed twilight, with
a soft sound of shuffling footsteps audible in
the motionless air.

And presently we also were prowling about
in this stealthy and silent fashion, regarding
the massive columns and porphyry pillars, the

bronze doors, the arabesques, the Biblical
stories writ large in mosaic, the dull golden
glow of the roof. But in walking about in
this fashion, little groups get separated, com-
mingle, separate again, so that the presence or
absence of any one person is hardly noticed.
Thus it was that when we came to leave the
building, we discovered that Amélie Dumaresq
was not with us : even Wolfenberg had not
observed her withdrawal — he had been so
much interested in this architectural treasure-
house.

But almost directly we discovered whither
she had gone. She was standing just outside
the door of the Cathedral, sketch-book in hand,
making a study, or pretending to do so, of a
withered little old man who was sweeping the
pavement. She was not alone. Paul Hitrovo
was standing by her, not overlooking her work,
but talking to her, while there was some
amusement visible in her face. They formed
quite a charming group, those two young

people : he, slender and elegant, with a certain careless grace of attitude and manner, perhaps a little conscious of his good looks—of his soft and silken brown hair, his small and neatly-waxed moustache, and his extraordinary blue-grey eyes ; she, of a more southern type, the long black lashes downcast as her glance came back from her model to her book, her manner almost shy, the exquisitely-formed lips smiling a little, her ungloved hands, small and plump and warm and white, looking somehow as if, were you to touch them, there would be a sudden shock, so full of vitality they seemed. She was not working very industriously ; she was listening, rather ; and she was pleased and amused. A very pretty group indeed they formed—in the cool shadow of the Cathedral, with the sunlit square beyond.

Wolfenberg hung back, as though he would rather not interrupt her ; but the rattling forward of our carriage attracted her attention, and at the same time she became aware that

we were awaiting her good pleasure. She
snapped the book to at once.

"Well," said she, brightly, as she took
her place in the carriage, "have you all of
you worshipped sufficiently at the shrine of
St. Gew-Gaw?"

"I feared you would not be impressed,
Amélie," Wolfenberg said, as we drove away :
the young Russian stood looking after us for
a moment or two, then he turned to his
companion : they seemed in no hurry to leave
this little town on the top of the hill.

"Impressed?" Miss Dumaresq said, almost
petulantly. "I was glad to get out into the
honest daylight. I cannot understand making
a place of worship a show-house, and imposing
on you with sham decoration. Now when
you go into a Gothic cathedral like Strassburg
or Cologne, you feel at once that there is
something about it noble, and simple, and
solemn, and reticent; but all that rococo
Byzantine splendour—and the tawdry magni-

ficence of the Renaissance churches—is to me insufferably sickening. Then if you come to those crude, stupid pictures in mosaic: I dare say they may be historically interesting; but you know very well, Ernest, that as Art they are mere monstrosities. But, above all, I hate to be treated like a child—I hate to be cheated——"

Wolfenberg (who seemed to have been a little serious as we came away from the Cathedral) now turned to the small woman who was in charge of us all; and there was a grave and good-humoured smile on his face.

"Won't you interpose?" he said. "There is one point on which Amélie and I never agree; and I can see she is coming to it. I think St. Mark's at Venice the most beautiful thing in the world. She thinks— what do you think, Amélie?"

Well, Miss Iconoclast had the courage of her convictions.

"St. Mark's in Venice," said she, calmly.
"Mr. Wolfenberg knows what I think of it.
It seems to me nothing but an enormous
sham—a pretence—pretty enough no doubt,
but a gigantic mass of deception. There is
not an ounce of solid reverent work in the
whole place; it is all veneer; it pretends to
be a marble building, whereas it is in reality
a brick building faced with marble; and now
that the thin slices are beginning to crack
and fall off, the truth is being revealed.
Trickery," she went on, more vehemently,
"is bad enough everywhere; but in a temple
it is particularly out of place. I don't wonder
there are winking Virgins when the church
is turned into a theatre to deceive people."
But here she suddenly stopped, with a very
pretty, and childish, and shamefaced little
laugh. "Ernest," she said, affecting to be
angry, "why did you lead me on to speak
of St. Mark's at Venice?"

"Why?" he answered her, with his usual

gentleness and indulgence. "Because our friends here must have learned by this time that ordinarily and almost always you have a singularly accurate and unbiassed mind, with clear perception, and frank judgment; and I wished them to see that all the same you could be as wildly unreasonable and prejudiced as any woman that ever breathed. I wanted to show that you were human, Amélie."

"Ah, you say that because you cannot defend veneer," she retorted, but she was laughing now, and in a fine good humour, and happy with herself and her surroundings. "That is your only answer. Well, we must agree to differ. And as St. Mark's is all tumbling into the mud, it's of very little consequence."

Then we drove away down into the valley, and through abundant orange groves, until we reached the gates leading to the Villa Tasca; and there, leaving both carriages

without, we entered the spacious grounds
that, in the absence of the beneficent proprietor, are thrown open to the public. And
here, amid all the luxuriance of tropical
foliage, amid the bewildering masses of
colour, and the statues, and miniature lakes
and fountains, it was quite delightful to see
how the nature of this child of the south
seemed to expand, as she drank in the hot,
spice-perfumed air. She was talking to every
one at once; she was trying to catch the swift-
darting lizards; she uttered little exclamations
of joyous surprise when opening vistas revealed
still further splendours of deep rose-red or
flaming scarlet. Peggy, on the other hand,
walked sedate and observant, listening civilly
and sweetly to the ever-attentive Major. The
tall, Juno-eyed Baby looked so grave and
majestic that we were almost ashamed of
ourselves for heeding these idle things of
the hour. There appeared to be no other
visitors in these beautiful gardens. Sappho

an.l her pug had stayed in the carriage; she preferred to await us there; and we had only to recall the derivation of the word cynosure to determine what occupied her undivided and admiring regard.

When we got back to the town, it seemed to be the universal wish of the women-folk to remain loitering about the sultry streets, for the reason that it would be some time before they got another opportunity of shopping; so—being of no manner of use to them, but rather in the way, indeed—we left them, under charge of the Major; and returned to the ship, and to the welcome shade of the awning. And thus it was that one happened to obtain a fuller knowledge of the peculiar relations that existed between Wolfenberg and Amélie Dumaresq; for here, on the deck of the deserted vessel, there was silence and privacy; and then, so careful was he of the smallest things that might affect her in the estimation of others, he seemed to fancy that some kind of apology was needful for her harsh treatment of St. Mark's.

"Downright honesty is her constant aim," he said, in his absent way, as if he were contemplating some creature of his imagination, before actually fixing it down with strokes of carbon. "She scorns pretence of any kind; and she has the courage to say what she thinks. . . . I suppose some people might find her character repellent. To me it is most attractive. But even if they found her repellent, they could not say she was uninteresting. She is too much of a living and breathing human being for that; she shows you too much of her personality; she may startle you and offend you, but at least you must be interested in her. . . ."

There was no response. Perhaps he did not expect any. At all events, he continued in the same preoccupied way, almost as if he were talking to himself:

" Her mind is downright, accurate, uncom- .
promising; she cannot tolerate illusions. And
that is why I sometimes think it is impossible·
she can ever become possessed by the greatest
and most terrible of all illusions—the idealism
of love. I do not think that will ever happen
to her. She sees too clearly. . . . She would
probably despise that idealisation and treat it
as mere sentiment. . . . And there again she
would be wrong. It is a tremendous force ;
the most powerful thing in the world—and
the most destructive. The delirium of love:
it is as intangible as frost; but it can do
more than merely split up rocks and cliffs :
it has split up empires—and ruined millions
of men's lives. . . . Some people seem even
to doubt its existence. . . . Exists ? You
may be sure that Mother Nature takes care
that it exists. She is cunning enough for
that. Why does she give a crimson tinge
to the rose-petal ? Why does she fill a young
man's head with ideals of maidenly beauty

and perfection, and persuade him that a rather commonplace young woman entirely corresponds to these, or even exceeds them ? . . . Of course he finds out in time. The wonderful angel is revealed to him as an ordinary creature of clay. But meanwhile Mother Nature has got *her* part done ; she has succeeded in *her* aim: the race is perpetuated. Whatever tragedy of disenchantment or repulsion may follow is no business of hers."

And here again one could say nothing, knowing the dark background there was to this man's life.

" No," he continued, " I do not think that Amélie Dumaresq could ever become the slave of a great passion. Her intelligence is too penetrating. Her mind is acute, accurate, observant—— "

" She is a woman."

" She is an artist. That way lies her ambition. Her interests are centred there.

Her plans of life have already been formed, and not without sufficient and earnest study. . . . Sometimes, indeed, I think you do not understand her yet. Probably you do not; it is hardly to be expected. You see her merry, laughing, childish, pleased with trifles. And that is all honest, mind you, absolutely honest : it is simply that she so completely and wholly enjoys every moment of living : to breathe the air—to look at a flower—to listen to a waltz—everything has a fascination for her. But that is only on the surface. Her nature is deeper and stronger than that. She is an artist; she has serious aims; this butterfly existence is pretty enough—and I for one am delighted to look on when she is in her gayest and most frivolous moods; but that is not Amélie Dumaresq. Her mother could tell you differently. Her mother could tell you of this girl sitting up till four in the morning, in the dead of winter, in front of a fire that had gone out dreaming and thinking of her work, her fingers almost frozen to the crayon, and yet hardly more than a suggestion or two put down on paper. For you must understand this : she is capable of idealisation ; only it is not the idealisation that would bewilder her senses and blind her in her choice of a husband, should such a thing ever happen, as I think it will not ; it is the idealisation that lends charm to the commonest objects she finds suited to her art. And it comes back to that : she has chosen her path in life, and nature has given her the means to follow it. Amélie Dumaresq is an artist—*au bout des ongles.*"

This he said, and a great deal more to the same effect, as he paced up and down the deck, sometimes looking across the water to the great bulk of Monte Pellegrino, that was now growing sombre in the warm evening light. And one could not avoid the suspicion that in these disjointed sentences—more disjointed than they are set down here—he was covertly seeking to persuade himself. His study of this girl's nature and character was, no doubt, the result of long observation ; and he had got the outlines firm enough ; only he seemed anxious to convince you—or to convince himself—that there could be nothing beyond and behind, that there were no other contingencies to be reckoned with. She was heart and soul an artist. She had with deliberation and foresight chosen her way of life. Her clear intellect, her uncompromising quest of truth, her scorn of unreality, were all safeguards against the illusions which might come in to disturb or destroy a woman's existence. He had forced himself to mention the possibility of her marriage, but only to dismiss it as unworthy of consideration. Amélie Dumaresq's position was defined ; he knew her, and could answer for her inmost thoughts ; her future he and she had planned together.

The evening waned, and still these women did not return. The vast amphitheatre of hills grew to be of a soft, deep rose-purple under the pale lemon-hued sky; and in the cool, grey twilight of the town one or two golden points had appeared just above the darkening sea. What had come over them? Mrs. Dumaresq was restless, and perturbed, and fretful. Not that she was apprehensive about her daughter's safety, but that it was close on the dinner-hour, and Amélie would not have time to change her dress.

"Come, let us go ashore and discover what has happened," Wolfenberg said.

But even as he spoke the steam-launch was seen to come round the point of the distant breakwater; and presently we could make out, even in this gathering dusk, that there were light-hued costumes on board. Nay, before the boat came alongside, it looked as though these people had armed themselves for some Bataille des Fleurs on the morrow, such a profusion of bouquets and baskets of flowers had they amongst them. Nor were they without abundant escort; for, besides the Major, they appeared to have picked up Paul Hitrovo and his companion; and the three gentlemen were all equally zealous in handing and carrying parcels and packages, while the women-folk managed their enormous bouquets as best they could.

Amélie Dumaresq was the first to arrive at the top of the gangway—breathless, laughing, her lips parted, her black eyes bright with excitement and pleasure.

"Oh, Ernest, how lazy of you!" she exclaimed. "Why, we have been everywhere, and seen everything!" Then she turned to her neighbour, who was the young Russian. "Here, Mr. Hitrovo, will you please take these flowers down to the saloon, and ask a steward to get some water for them, and put them on our table? Oh, thank you!"

She took from him the parcels he had been

holding for her; and the dinner bell had already begun to tinkle in the forward part of the ship when she hurried away to make some hasty alterations in her attire.

CHAPTER VI.

"VIX E CONSPECTU SICULÆ TELLURIS."

THE new day has not yet come; nevertheless we seem to have emerged from the night—it lies behind us low and sullen along the west; while the great ship labouring onwards through this mysterious twilight has over its foretop-mast the silver crescent of the moon, as if we were bearing with us, into the East, the symbol of the East. In the north are the Æolian islands, Volcano, Lipari, and their lonely neighbours; but they also are dark and over-shadowed; Vulcan and his Cyclopes have not yet lit their forges; from those distant conical peaks arises no wavering tongue of pink, no column of lurid smoke. But all the same light is coming: the never-failing, never-

familiar wonders of the dawn are near. As
one regards this livid and slaty-black sea, here
and there a liquid crest is touched with a dull
saffron ; ahead of us the dim coast-line—a
mere film of land along the horizon—gradually
becomes of a transparent olive-green; and
above that again the sky is a glow of ruddy
gold that is rendered all the more intense by
one long, far-stretching cloud of the deepest
and softest violet, its warm, rich tones of an in-
describable beauty. The over-arching heavens
are now of a lambent, tremulous silver-grey :
the sickle of the moon still reigns placidly
there. Swiftly and silently the morning
splendour spreads and grows; the great violet
cloud has turned to an exquisite rose-purple,
with fringes of crimson fire ; then, of a sudden,
over the rim of the land, appears the blinding
edge of the sun ; a shiver of light seems to
spring through the sleeping world ; and as one
turns to see what bewildering miracle has been
wrought, behold ! far away over there in the

south the pale snows of Etna have already answered to the flame.

And here, up at the bow of the vessel, a group of early risers have clustered together, some idly chattering, others gazing abroad on the new world of sea and sky and ever-approaching land. Wolfenberg stands somewhat apart, silent and alone, apparently plunged in a profound reverie. Amélie Dumaresq, with her laughing and lustrous black eyes full of interest, is listening to the tall young Russian, who, in his turn, seems trying, lazily and smilingly, to amuse her. The rotund and roseate Major has got hold of a plateful of biscuits, and is bustling about with these, perhaps unconsciously selecting the prettiest of the young women for his favours. But who is it who forms the principal, the most attractive feature of this miscellaneous throng —who but our shining-eyed, and peerless, and radiant Peggy ? As usual, Peggy has climbed to a commanding post; her outstretched right arm, holding on to the foretopmast-stay, reveals to fine advantage her slender and elegant figure; the simple, tight-fitting grey dress looks well against the pale blue of the sky; she has no covering on her head, so that the sunlight makes a wonder of her neatly-plaited, light-brown hair. And as for her face?—well, she appears to be entirely happy and content with herself, as if she were ready to smile if her regard met any one; but she is not heeding those around her; she is looking away across the flashing and surging waves to the transparent line of coast. Many and many a ship, in all ages of the world, has sailed these well-known waters, but never one of them with such a glorified figure at the prow.

And was not this a grand and notable day for the Passionate Poetess? She was so breathlessly excited, so busy with her dog's-eared translations and her Lempriere, that she had not yet found time to pay her morning call on the butcher, to fetch her beloved

Phaon. For were not these now receding peaks the mysterious abode of the Ruler of the Winds? She had got hold of the *hic vasto rex Æolus antro* passage ; and as she marched up and down the deck, we could hear her repeating to herself some high-sounding line—

Luctantes ventos, tempestatesque sonoras,

or

Illi indignantes magno cum murmure montis,

or the like. And was she not following in the wake of her favourite Ulysses? Ahead of us were Scylla and Charybdis, and Cape Pelorum, and the famous Straits along which every hamlet and town and river recalls some old-world legend or some tragic historical event. At the same time it was not all joy for Sappho. The discrepancies she found in those various authors, even in such minor matters as spelling, chafed her spirit; and her indignant protests, accompanied even by a little show of ill-temper, were addressed indiscriminately to any one who would listen

—even to the Major, poor man, who solemnly assured her that he had not construed a single verse of Greek or Latin since he left school.

"It's their horrible inconsistencies!" she exclaimed; and at times she appeared almost ready to take refuge in tears. "One book tells you that the Cyclopes lived on the coast of Libya, and another says the west of Sicily, and another under Mount Etna. As for the island of the Sirens, they seem to put it just wherever they like; but I suppose it really must have been over by Cape Pelorus, since Ulysses, after getting past it, came immediately on Scylla and Charubdis. Scylla and Charybdis!" she went on, bitterly, for here was another grievance. "Oh, no, not at all—not at all! Skūllê and Charubdis! Skūllê! what *is* the use of such tomfoolery! And Kirke, and Kalūpso, and the Kuklopes! And I'd like to know how they ever got Odysseus changed into Ulysses; and more than that, when they had got it changed, and accepted by all the world, what good is there in going back, not to Odysseus, but to Odūsseus? It is such preposterous folly!"

Yet worse, far worse, remained behind: something calculated to strike dismay into the stoutest heart. For at this moment the Baby came up, carrying a binocular glass in her hand; and, with shy good-nature, she said——

"Would you like my glass, Miss Penguin? They say that rock over there is Scylla."

"Scylla?" said Sappho, with something of a start—for indeed the tall grey rock was visible to the naked eye. "That Scylla? There must be some mistake! For in the Odyssey it says that the rock reaches to the heavens, and has perpetual clouds on the top of it. And—and Charybdis?"

Instinctively she turned to look at the other shore—perhaps with a dreadful doubt possessing her. Well, what she saw was simply this : a breadth of calm blue sea, shimmering in the sunlight, with the slightest of ripples; and beyond that a very pleasant and smiling coast-line, with strips of yellow-grey villages, and over these a series of vineyard-terraced hills. But as for Scylla the awful monster ?—and divine Charybdis sucking in black water thrice a day, and sending it out again, and defying even the dread might of Poseidon ? Sappho was silent : she would not confess to the terrible fear that she had been beguiled. And when one pointed out to her that in stormy weather the narrow entrance into these Straits of Messina might be quite dangerous enough for any small sailing vessel, she still remained silent. And then she went away to ask for Phaon.

However, any doubts about the literal trustworthiness of Homer that might have clouded her mind for a moment would seem to have been soon forgotten; for some little time thereafter Peggy came along in a very secret and solemn manner, and intimated that she had a matter of importance to communicate.

"It's a poem," said Peggy.

"What about?"

"Ulysses passing the island of the Sirens. Oh, I assure you it is tremendous. Do you know what Sappho herself says?—she says 'Fling a few burning words into the air: they are more than all the philosophies: they will sound in the hearts of men through the ages.'"

"Has she flung them?"

"I have them in my pocket."

"Let me see them!"

But here Peggy hesitates, and looks round.

"The Baby is over there," she says, with an uneasy glance, "and she always insists that it is very wrong to have secrets. It is undignified. If she saw me handing you this paper, and waiting for you to read it, she would be shocked. That's what it is to have a severe and superior being for a sister—even though she's not long out of school——"

"Oh, nonsense——"

"I'll tell you what I will do; I will get an envelope, and enclose the poem, and leave it for you in the Purser's office: then you can go for it and read the verses at your leisure."

"Sweet simplicity—that would be a pretty stratagem for the Baby to discover! What? —is your guilty soul so sensitive that you cannot take a bit of poetry out of your pocket and show it in open daylight! What have you been doing? Have you been bewildering the Major?"

"Oh, let the Major alone—as I do!" she says. "Suppose we go and sit down by the wheel-box: then you need not be interrupted."

And thus it is that one becomes possessed,

temporarily, of the following burning words
—which are hereby flung into the air.
Whether they will sound through the ages
it is obviously not for the present transitory
race of men to determine.—

Brothers, I hear the Siren sing,
Where by Pelorus the white waves spring:
My pulses raven, my senses swirl—
O could I clutch thee, goddess or girl!

Unbind me, ye fools, that made me fast,
Ere with my sinews I break the mast!
Astarte, Astarte, grant me breath!
Astarte, Astarte, help or death!

Slaves and dotards, why stand ye there?
The music swims through the shivering air:
Curses upon ye, unbind these arms!
What know ye of love's fierce hurts and harms!

Pale Penelope, fare you well—
We meet no more upon this side Hell:
Farewell to the shining Cyclades—
I end my life in the Sirens' seas.

Nay, loose me, ye fools, that bound me fast,
Ere with my sinews I break the mast!
Astarte, Astarte, grant me breath!—
Astarte, Astarte, love or death!

" Well!" says Peggy.

"Her geography seems a little shaky : does she imagine that Ithaca is among the shining Cyclades ? "

"Oh, how mean ! Now that is just like a critic ! You take exception to a quite unimportant detail, and miss all the fiery spirit of the piece itself ! "

"There is plenty of fiery spirit, no doubt : double-distilled fusel-oil is a fool to it. What are you going to do with the trash ? "

"Yes, I always did think men were more envious than women," Peggy says, rather sadly, as she takes the shred of MS., and folds it up, and returns it to her pocket. "Because you can't do a certain thing yourself you needn't belittle it when it is done by some one else. And, after all, she is only acting up to her own contention—that there should be more passion in modern poetry. . . . Well, now, I can get away without the Baby suspecting any secret confabulation. Good-bye for the present."

This was a pleasant morning we had for our leisurely sail along the eastern coast of Sicily : a Rhine-looking country, with ruddy-grey hills sprinkled with green ; here and there a yellow-white village extending along the shore ; an occasional ruined tower perched high on a pinnacle of rock, overlooking the glassy water. Then as we got further to the south the vast domain of Etna began to declare itself ; the great mountain visible from sea-base to summit ; on the lower slopes innumerable houses like grains of sand shining among the dark foliage of the orange groves ; the higher slopes ruddy and scarred ; the far-receding cone sprinkled with snow. Almost too majestic a background, perhaps, for the trivial human interests that were being interwoven on board this ship ? Yet these had to be considered ; in fact, they were thrust upon us.

For, first of all, Mrs. Dumaresq, seizing a favourable opportunity, came and sat down by the side of our Mrs. Threepenny-bit ; and after a little anxious beating about the bush, began to speak about M. Paul Hitrovo, and to ask us what we knew of him. Well, we knew nothing of him, or next to nothing. But this elderly woman, with the sallow face, sad eyes, and braided silver-white hair, seemed concerned and perturbed ; she said that every one must have observed the marked attention the young Russian was now paying to her daughter ; and she lamented that Amélie was so wilful and self-confident that it was of no use to speak to her or to caution her.

"The only one she might heed would be Mr. Wolfenberg," said the distressed mother. "But how is it possible to speak to him about so delicate a matter ? Of course he has noticed. I have seen him look at them. But then he is very proud ; he would not claim anything on account of the great friendship that has existed for so long between Amélie and himself ; he would rather stand aside, and leave her to do as she pleases. Of course I say nothing against Mr. Hitrovo, for I know nothing ; and —and they say he is very well connected ; but it would be dreadful if Amélie were to get herself seriously entangled, and then we were to find out something against him.   I don't know what to do.   Ernest Wolfenberg has always advised us ; but in this matter, somehow, I cannot go to him—I cannot. And I dare not warn Amélie ; she would demand to know what ground I have for any suspicions.   And I have none."

" Supposing," one ventures to suggest to her, " that when we get to Constantinople some one could be found who might good-naturedly make inquiries at the Russian Embassy, would you consider that indiscreet ? "

" But I am an American ; and I do not know that there is an American Minister at Constantinople," she said.

" In any case it might be managed through the British Embassy, with a little diplomacy."

"I am so unwilling to do anything without consulting Mr. Wolfenberg," said this poor mother, who seemed to feel her own helplessness acutely. "And yet, as I say, it is impossible to speak to him. And if Amélie knew that I have even mentioned such a matter to any one, she would be most indignant and angry. She would say I was compromising her—insulting her. Then she is so headstrong. Most likely any interference would only drive her in the opposite direction. Yet who can avoid remarking it? There is not a word now about her painting. She seems to have forgotten entirely what she came away for. Formerly, Mr. Wolfenberg and she had subjects to speak of all day long; he was always showing her something, teaching her something; and her great ambition when she came away on this vessel was to get on with oil-colours as a change from the water. But now there is not a syllable about that. The Russian follows her like her shadow; and I think at

the same time he tantalises her with a kind of
indifference that she is not used to. He rather
patronises her in that smiling way of his, and
almost expects her to amuse him. Amélie
does not understand it; it piques her and
pleases her; it is a new sensation. So you
think you may find out something about him
at Constantinople ?"

"It is at least possible."

"Oh, thank you, thank you !" she said, very
gratefully—and she rose to go away, as if
fearing that the subject of this conversation
might be guessed at by some passer-by.
"And not a word to Mr. Wolfenberg, please !"
she added, in an earnest undertone. "It
would only pain him unnecessarily, and he
is so sensitive, especially where Amélie is
concerned. Well, I had hoped for other things
from this voyage." And the poor woman left
with a sigh—stealing away guiltily, as it were;
though it was only a nervous apprehension and
anxiety about her daughter's happiness that

had driven her to this timid confession and appeal.

Our next experience on this eventful morning was of a more cheerful cast. We discovered that we had got a stranger on board. Now, when we left Tilbury the great majority of the Orotanians were entirely unacquainted with each other; but this constant association, day after day, had so familiarised us with each other's appearance that the sudden advent of an unknown person seemed a startling thing. Not that there was anything alarming or forbidding about the newcomer; on the contrary, his air and manner were most prepossessing; and if his costume struck us as strange—it was clearly a land-travelling costume—perhaps that was merely because he had not yet had time to open his sea-kit. He was a young fellow of about two-and-twenty, quite boyish in look, fresh-complexioned, with hardly the semblance of a moustache, and with such an expression of

modest ingenuousness as at once bespoke
favour. We first noticed him at breakfast-
time. Now on board the *Orotania* it was
only at dinner that fixed places were kept;
at breakfast and lunch any one coming into
the saloon took any seat that happened to be
vacant, just as is done at a club. When this
English-looking lad appeared at the door of
the saloon, he glanced round with quite a
pretty shyness. There did chance to be one
vacant chair at our table; and it was near
him; he made a faltering step towards it—
hesitated—seemed to be overcome with diffi-
dence and embarrassment—and then went on
in vague quest of an empty corner. The odd
thing was that this momentary hesitation on
his part seemed to have had an instant and
curious effect on the Baby—our serious and
solemn-eyed and self-possessed Baby—who
was now blushing furiously; she even looked
frightened. But supposing he had actually
sat down at the table, what cataclysm could

possibly have ensued ? On board our excellent *Orotania* ham and eggs are free to all: to each man his share, no one grudging. Nor could the Baby have complained of being taken unawares by a stranger; for as to the smallest details of her toilet she was always and invariably diligent and scrupulous at the earliest hour; on this particular morning, long before we had come to terrible Scylla and the divine Charybdis, she had come up on deck dressed as if for an afternoon drive.

Thereafter, as we sailed along the Sicilian shores, the modest youth rather kept himself out of the way, though his 'landward' costume made him more or less conspicuous. He did not venture to speak to any of the passengers. Nor did he seem to care much about the coast we were passing; though surely such names as Taormina, Aci Reale, Catania, Mount Hybla, and Megara were calculated to awaken visions and dreams. And at length one or two of our more curious brethren made bold

to go to the Purser, to demand information
about the mysterious newcomer. His name?
That, at least, could be ascertained—Julian
Verrinder. What?—of the Verrinders of
Devon? Mr. Purser was unable to say: all
he knew was that the young man had tele-
graphed from Naples to the London Office of
the Company to see if he could have a cabin,
and that he came on board the previous
evening, at Palermo. What further? Why,
nothing. Moreover, the young man, in holding aloof, kept away forward by the engines,
walking up and down there, and seemingly
not disposed to enter into conversation with
any one. It is true that once or twice, when
our attention happened to be withdrawn from
that absorbingly interesting coast-line, it
seemed to one of us that the young stranger
sometimes threw a furtive and timid glance
in our direction; but that may have been
mere fancy; anyway, there was enough now
ahead of us to occupy our eyes.

For here was a long spur of land coming out into the blue sea, covered with a white, flat-roofed, Eastern-looking town, and ending in a battlemented fort. This was Syracuse; rather, this was Ortygia; and the sheet of smooth green water opening out before us was the Great Harbour in which Athens met her doom. Now, callous as any one may be about the woes of Hecuba, it is surely impossible to sail into the Bay of Syracuse without recalling, with actual and vivid compassion and pity, the tremendous tragedy that was here enacted. Ordinary battlefields are rarely impressive—are rarely intelligible. Their distinctive features are soon obliterated. The present writer, at all events, has never been able to make even a guess at what has happened on such and such a modern battle-field, unless, indeed, it chanced that certain heaps of dead bodies lying about, of men and horses, appeared to show where a stand had been made against a charge of cavalry.

But in the case of Syracuse and its wide harbour, all the necessary points are easy of identification: nay, it seems as if it might have been only the other day that Etna, looking down from the north, beheld the overwhelming rout and slaughter of the environed Greeks, and heard the wild weeping and piteous exclamations of their companions along the shore, who knew that for them also remained nothing but the agony of a hopeless flight, and capture, and death. Yonder, at the other extremity of the horseshoe bay, Cape Plemmyrium; here, at this nearer point, Ortygia ; stretching away upward, the heights of Epipolæ, where, on that ghostly moonlight night, Demosthenes had almost recovered the desperate fortunes of his countrymen, when the very Gods seemed to intervene to drive them back to destruction ; and finally, in front of us, between us and the shore, the placid sheet of shining green water—the scene of a still more awful fight—the last effort of the

Athenian ships to break out of the chained and stockaded bay—the death-struggle that ended in the most tragic defeat, and the most cruel tale of prolonged and merciless suffering, known to history. The tears of Hecuba were shed long ago, and do not much concern us now ; but not even the most trivial and careless of travellers can sail into the harbour of Syracuse without being in a measure overawed by the recollection of the stupendous overthrow of the great Athenian armaments. That which broke the power of Athens and ultimately wrought her ruin cannot easily be forgotten by the civilised world.

But all the same we were glad to find our good, dear, impetuous Sappho in a most eager and buoyant humour. She had got upon the track of Ulysses at last ; indeed, she had pinned him into a corner ; there was no further escape for him now. Hitherto the wanderings of the much-enduring hero had caused her infinite perplexity, nay, had even

ruffled her temper in a way we were pained
to witness; while the glosses and guesses of
translators had only driven her to still direr
distraction. But now she had narrowed the
issues to a point; she had Ulysses by the
throat, as it were.

"Look at this," said she, triumphantly, as
she produced one of those volumes of Bohn that
get so rapidly shabby on board ship. "When
Ulysses escapes from Scylla and Charybdis,
he sails along the coast of the island until
his companions persuade him to land; and
then he says, 'We stationed the well-made
ship in the hollow port, near the sweet water.'
Now, that *must* have been Syracuse—this
very bay; and as for the sweet water, obviously it is the Fountain of Arethusa, over
there behind the trees. Could anything be
more accurate, more interesting? Isn't it
strange that Homer should have known
about that fountain of sweet water?" Indeed,
she was overjoyed by this discovery; and

went about proclaiming it ; and we were quite
pleased to see the venerable goddess so delighted.

But the mention of a fountain had fallen
on Amélie Dumaresq's ear. She, like the rest
of us, was in the forward part of the vessel,
looking at those yellow houses and the green
palms and oleanders, and waiting for the roar
of the anchor. And she had been talking
to Paul Hitrovo. But on hearing something
said about a fountain, she turned suddenly
to Wolfenberg, who was standing by, a little
way apart.

"Ernest," said she, in accents of gay reproach, as she went over to him, "it has just
occurred to me: why have you told me
nothing further about your picture ? Have
you forgotten it ? Have you abandoned it ?
All these days, and not a word ! You do
not mean to say that we are to have no
Fountain of Callirrhoe ? "

The man with the pale, worn face, and the

pensive and absent eyes, flushed a little: perhaps he did not care to have his work spoken of before strangers.

"These last few days?—I have not been thinking of it," he made answer, in the gentle tone he invariably adopted towards her; but at the same time he seemed rather to move away somewhat; and she, after a moment's surprise, returned to her Russian friend.

CHAPTER VII.

THE EAR OF DIONYSIUS.

OF a sudden all this was changed. Just as
we were about to set out for the shore, Amélie
Dumaresq was again consigned to our care;
and as that necessitated the choice of a fourth
to make up our driving-party, Mrs. Threepenny-bit promptly invited Wolfenberg to
accompany us: she would have no Russian
hanging about, with dangerous complications
in the background. And so far from Amélie
Dumaresq resenting this arrangement, she
seemed to welcome it; and no sooner had we
landed from the steam-launch, and got ourselves into the ramshackle vehicle that was
to drive us round the environs of Syracuse,
than it became obvious she was bent on

pleasing and captivating all her companions, but especially Ernest Wolfenberg. Perhaps she was secretly conscious that she had of late neglected him; perhaps she had noticed him standing about the deck very much by himself; perhaps she had remarked that his stern, grave face appeared to be graver, his dreamy eyes more absent and wistful than was their wont. At all events, it looked as though she was now determined to make ample atonement. As we drove away from this sweltering harbour she was in the gayest and friendliest of good-humours. Her own content and gladness seemed to radiate from her; the clear Sicilian atmosphere lent animation to the pale olive hue of her satin-soft cheek; her liquid black eyes (as black as her magnificent blue-black hair) danced in audacious merriment; when that rosebud of a mouth smiled, even in wicked satire, it was difficult to deny sympathetic acquiescence. Moreover, she was merciful to us on this occasion. She did not frighten us out of our wits with startling paradoxes or ruthless iconoclasm. For her, she was quite moderately wilful, and petulant, and self-assertive. And when she spoke to Wolfenberg it was with a gentleness, and consideration, and even a subtle and insidious flattery that entirely merited approval.

And as for him? Well, it was in its way pathetic to see this man—so immeasurably her superior in intellectual and artistic endowments; so immeasurably her superior, also, in qualities of character—it was almost pathetic to see how grateful he was to her for this kindness and attention to him. Not that he betrayed his gratitude in any sentimental fashion; on the contrary, he kept laughing at her perversities and vagaries, and kept interposing here and there to make little explanations or apologies for her. Sometimes, indeed, a certain callousness on her part appeared to grate against his finer sense;

but all the same he would defend her, or
perhaps remonstrate with her in the most
delicate fashion. For example, she was making merry, making rather maliciously merry,
over our good, dear Sappho—over her appearance, her dress, her pug, her passionate poetry,
her Lempriere erudition, and what not; and
she went on to declare that on this very
morning she had heard Miss Penguin express
the wish that she might get back from the
fort of Eury'alus in time to take a boat
and go up the An'apus in order to get some
leaves of the pap'yrus. All through this
Wolfenberg had looked rather uncomfortable.
For if a woman has sandy hair, how can she
help it? And a heavy and lethargic face
may accompany a brilliant and penetrative
mind. A dowdy dress does not necessarily
indicate a cruel or envious disposition. As
for errors in accentuation—

"Don't you think, Amélie," said Wolfenberg
in his timidly suggestive way, "that where

there is no pretence, the blunders of ignorance are very venial things?—don't you think they rather call for sympathy and silence? Eury'alus is a quite natural mistake."

"Look here, Ernest," said she, abruptly breaking away from the subject, for she did not like being reproved, even by him, "why don't you paint a portrait of Lady Cameron? —she is the beauty of the ship."

"Why don't you do it yourself, Amélie?" he suggested.

"Oh, I?" she said with a frank laugh. "I brutalise everything I touch. You would make a dream of it. This morning, at sunrise, when we were coming near to the Straits of Messina, did you notice her up at the bow —perched away above the rest of us as usual; and when the light came over from the east, her face seemed to me quite mystically beautiful. It was a vision; it was something for you, Ernest, I tell you. Of course that is a trick of hers, getting up high: she knows

she has a fine figure. And swinging her
Tam o' Shanter in her hand is another; she
likes to be bare-headed, because her hair
shows well in the sunlight. But I am not
jealous; I don't bear malice; I love beautiful
things, whether they are alive or merely
marble. Only, what I say is, you ought
not to lose the opportunity. If you don't
wish to paint her portrait, at least make
studies of her head: you will rarely meet
with such a model. Why, you have not
done a stroke of work since you left England!"

"Have you?" said he, with a smile.

"You must not talk like that," said she,
a little proudly. "Your work and mine are
not quite on the same plane—no, not quite!
My manufacture I can turn out at any
moment; and if I have been idle, it has
been because there was too much to look at,
too much to interest. But I should not
have expostulated with you, Ernest. I
know how your work comes to you better

than you do yourself. It is exactly what Shelley says about poetry : ' Poetry is the record of the best and happiest moments of the best and happiest minds ' . . . ' evanescent visitations of thought and feeling ' . . . ' arising unforeseen and departing unbidden.' Your work is inspiration ; my daubs are mechanical——— "

"Amélie ! " said he—but whether he was protesting against her skilful flattery or against her self-depreciation we could not quite make out.

"Oh, do you think I don't know ?" she exclaimed. "I tell you I understand how your work comes to you ; it is a sudden fancy, and if you do not seize it and hold it, it is off again, and you care no more about it. Ernest, have you let the Fountain of Callirrhoe slip away like that ? "

"I hardly know," he said, rather uneasily. "How can one tell ? It was, as you say, a passing fancy ; and when one is thinking of other things one forgets." He shifted the subject: he turned to our Mrs. Threepenny-bit (who would have been quite content to hear those two go on talking, with her own speculations making an inward commentary). "Do you notice how delicious a colour green is, after we have come through long days of blinding blue and silver?" (For this dusty roadway we were driving along was bordered by an abundance of fresh vegetation —bananas, lemons, pomegranates, the last showing their waxen fruit taking a tinge of crimson on their sunward side). "It is a kind of feast for the eyes: I did not know one's sight had grown so hungry. Yet blue and silver—Mediterranean blue and brilliant sunlight—are welcome enough at the time."

She did not answer him; for at this moment the driver drew up in front of a gate; and we were expected to descend. We discovered that this was the entrance to the waste land surrounding the ruins of the Roman Amphitheatre; and here we found one or two of our excellent Orotanians wandering about, picking up flowers, or gazing down at the remains of the ancient building and its adjuncts—the terraced stone seats, the alligator tanks, the massive cages for the wild beasts, all of which seemed as though they had been used but yesterday, so perfect were they. And this was not a gloomy spectacle like the Coliseum at Rome; this was set amid fair lemon groves and verdant vineyards, all smiling in the warm afternoon sun.

Paul Hitrovo was here, along with his Monreale friend. He observed Miss Dumaresq come into these grounds, but made no motion of approach; she also threw a glance —one might almost say a furtive glance— in his direction, but affected to be entirely absorbed in conversation with her companion. Indeed, she was arm-in-arm with Mrs. Threepenny-bit; and was very affectionate; and was apologising for having taken the place of Lady Cameron on these our landward excursions. And when we came away again she still clung in this familiar fashion to her chaperon, and had no eyes for any one else, save when she turned to address a friendly word to Wolfenberg from time to time; and in this manner, having ordered the carriage to follow, we went forward on foot towards our next objective point—the so-called Ear of Dionysius.

We left the road, and went along a deep-descending wooded dell; we found in front of us a lofty mass of rock, thick-hanging with ivy; we entered by a wooden door in a low stone wall; and then the mysterious twilight told us we were in a vast cave, the further recesses of which, as well as the vault overhead, were invisible in the impenetrable gloom. And what was this strange " swish ! —swish !" we heard all around, and above, and far beyond ?—what but our own footsteps ! We discovered that the faintest sound we could make—the light snapping of one's fingers, the rustling of a piece of paper— was carried away from us, and repeated again and again in the distant and obscure unknown; while the door behind us, when it was slammed to by the military custodian, sent thundering reverberations that seemed to plunge howling and rolling into the very bowels of the earth. And who were these who now approached us, coming out of the opaque darkness into the trembling, uncertain light ? The roseate and beaming Major—our gracious and smiling Lady of Inverfask—the tall, grave, goddess-eyed Baby : it was a welcome meeting.

"This place seems full of ghosts," said Peggy, in an awe-stricken way. "If you speak to any one, they whisper all round you."

"Gad," said the Major, " I should not like to have been one of the prisoners shut up here by that old tyrant. Precious little sleep for them, I should think. Now let us go out-side and get away up to the gallery where he used to sit and listen and discover their secrets."

But we late-comers did not mean to lose so invaluable a guide ; for the Major had been in Sicily and in Syracuse oftentimes before ; so we attached our party to his, and together we passed out into the warmer air. On our way up to the road again, Wolfenberg gathered a few fronds of maidenhair fern, and offered them to Amélie Dumaresq. She accepted them, and looked pleased. The old comradeship seemed to be re-established between those two.

Now, to reach the little gallery and chamber which legend maintains Dionysius had constructed so that, by the curious acoustic properties of this immense cavern, he might overhear his prisoners talking, you have to climb away up to the top of the Greek Theatre—an imposing ruin, of far

greater extent than the Roman Amphitheatre. And when we came in sight of
that far-stretching, far-rising, yellow-grey pile
of horse-shoe terraced stone seats, about the
first thing we noticed was two figures making
for the summit. Very small they looked in
that great space ; but by their white costumes
and puggarees we knew them to be Orotanians ; and the next moment we had recog-
nised them—they were the young Russian
and his companion. Well, why not? Had
they not as much right to go sight-seeing as
anybody ? Nay, had they not even seemed to
avoid us, by coming past the cave without
seeking to enter ?

But when we had clambered up these
century-worn tiers, and crossed a space of
gritty ground and spiky weeds, and come to
an opening cut into the rock leading to the
higher end of the cavern, we found that M.
Hitrovo had not the least wish to avoid us.
On the contrary, he rather left his companion,

and came forward, and spoke pleasantly and carelessly to this one and that, eventually, however, addressing himself exclusively to Amélie Dumaresq. And, oddly enough, he invariably seemed to have the power of drawing her away from her friends—if only for a yard or so—so that he 'and she could speak together. Yet there was no affectation of secresy; not at all. She appeared to find him amusing. She would look at him with her eyes full of smiles. As for him, he did not seem to take too much trouble about her. He rather patronised her. But he had a pretty laugh; and his eyes—yes, it could not be denied that those blue-grey eyes were singularly clear, that they were full of light, and that they might possibly have a bewildering effect on a young woman become curious and interested.

At this moment Peggy came back from the opening into the rock.

" What we should have done," said she,

"was for one of us to have remained in the cavern. Here we can talk into the roof of the place, but there is no one to answer us from below."

"Oh, I will go down if you like," said Paul Hitrovo at once. "What do you say, Miss Dumaresq? Shall we go down and listen to them and answer them?"

"Oh, yes, yes, by all means," said she, cheerfully; and the next moment those two were making their way down the successive stone ridges of this great theatre, in the direction of the distant road, and the aque-duct, and chasm leading to the echoing cave. It was all the work of an instant. How was any one to interfere? Or was Amélie Dumaresq the kind of person to brook inter-ference?

But Mrs. Threepenny-bit, whose attention had been drawn away at the moment, was most angry and indignant when she discovered what had happened. Those two retreating figures had now reached the aqueduct; another second, and they had disappeared from sight.

"It is really too bad," she said, with frowning brows. "She is under my charge. She has no right to make off like that. If she has had her head turned—— "

She stopped. Wolfenberg was standing by. But indeed he was not listening. There was a strange look on his features. His eyes were pre-occupied and thoughtful, but the eyebrows were drawn down somewhat; and the firm mouth that gave character to an otherwise wistful and pensive countenance betokened determination. Was he nerving himself to face something he had not hitherto contemplated? Or was he merely resolved to pay no heed to this little incident that had just occurred? Apparently, he was not looking after the fugitives—though he must have seen them disappear; his gaze, at once absent and inscrutable, was fixed on that fertile champaign country with its luxuriant lemon groves, and on the yellow-grey city perched on the point, with the fair blue-belt of sea beyond. He did not seem to wish to speak to any one. He was alone with himself—and we left him so.

What echo-borne conversation ensued between the little group in this small and lofty gallery and the two unseen people in the profound abyss below, we did not care to hear : for one thing, there was a cold wind coming whistling through that aperture sufficiently dangerous for folk who had been all day baked and boiled and blistered under a Sicilian sun. The remarkable circumstance was that Hitrovo and Amélie Dumaresq did not reappear—even after this experiment was long over. The carriages were in sight down by the aqueduct ; but those two made no sign.

" We'd better go down," said Mrs. Three-penny-bit, concealing her vexation very well indeed. " Most likely they are waiting for us, or perhaps they may have set out on foot for Syracuse without saying anything—young people are so inconsiderate."

However, when we had descended those massive steps, and when we had got into the road, and round by the aqueduct, we thought we might as well have a look at the winding chasm leading to the cave; and here, indeed, we found the two truants, strolling about, and apparently quite unconcerned. Amélie Dumaresq was carrying a nosegay of various wild flowers. No doubt they had been gathered for her by her companion. And the modest little tribute of maiden-hair fern that Wolfenberg had presented her with? That was gone. Well, ferns wither soon; perhaps she had thrown them away. But an odd thing happened with regard to this new and more florid bouquet. The soldier in charge of the Orecchio di Dionisio had come along to bid us good-bye (perhaps with some ulterior views) and the moment he caught

sight of the nosegay he said to her in his
mangled and guttural French :

" Mademoiselle, you have there some poison-
ous flowers ; they will do injury to your hands.
See, I will show you the bad ones."

For a second she did not quite catch his
meaning ; but when she did she saved him all
the trouble of separation ; she instantly flung
the whole lot away with a gesture as if she
had already been stung.   For Miss Dumaresq,
as we had noticed before now, had a pretty
good idea of taking care of .herself.   As we
drove away back to Syracuse, she repeatedly
looked at the palm and fingers of her little
plump white hand.   And she had abundant
opportunities of doing so ; for Wolfenberg was
unusually silent ; when he spoke, it was mostly
to Mrs. Threepenny-bit, as we sometimes call
her.

That night, after dinner, Amélie Dumaresq
was entirely in her element.   There was music
on the Marina ; the town was all illuminated ;

from the deck of the ship you could see the electric light shining on the tall white houses; there were the black masses of the acacia-trees along the promenade; then there were the long lines of silver reflections quivering on the glassy water. The music was gay waltz-music; it was all pretty, modern, French, light-hearted; she, lying back in her chair, and looking towards the shore, might have fancied herself at Biarritz, at Nice, at Monte Carlo. She was chattering away vivaciously. Would it not make an excellent Impressionist subject—the spectral houses, the dark masses of the trees, the blue-white globes, the quivering of the reflected lights down through the black deeps? She would like to try it herself—in oils, when she had grown more familiar with that medium.

"What do you say, Ernest?" she asked, looking round, for Wolfenberg was standing by.

"Whatever you see your way to doing,

Amélie," he made answer, "will have character and quality in it—and life."

Only one other occurrence remains to be
chronicled of this evening ; but that was of a
wholly cataclysmic nature. The humble re-
porter of these various doings and proceedings,
having been sent down to the saloon to order
some "cold sodas" for the women-folk, was
returning to his place, when he chanced to run
against a young lady who was standing in the
dusky shadow outside the top of the companion-
way. And with every wish to be discreet, and
blind, and non-existent, he could not but perceive that the young lady had just received,
and was now quickly thrusting into her pocket,
some scrap of paper that had been handed
her by a young gentleman who was making
off in another direction. The young man,
clearly enough, was Julian Verrinder, who had
come on board at Palermo in that curiously
unaccountable fashion, apparently without any
pre-arranged purpose, and professing to know

no human creature in the ship. The young
woman——oh, Baby, Baby !

*   *   *   *   *

Next morning was devoted to busy idleness.
Some went off on an exploration of the older
portions of Ortygia—though that was rather a
difficult undertaking, many of the thoroughfares
being so narrow that when you met a drove of
donkeys they had to be turned into the houses
and the cellar-like wineshops to let you go by;
others got a boat and made away for the River
Anapus; while one or two of us thought we
would stroll along to the Fountain of Arethusa
—chiefly to fall in with the burning impetuosity
and entreaties of our good Sappho. And as
Lady Cameron went with us, so, you may
be sure, did the ever-faithful Major. And
here, too, was the Baby—the serious, the
reserved, Juno-eyed maiden, whose very
manner was a standing reproach to her more
sprightly sister. As for the young man who
had mysteriously sprung himself upon us after

leaving Palermo—— But he was nowhere to be seen.

And it must be owned that on this occasion the Major behaved himself in a most shocking fashion; for irreverence is not becoming to advanced years. He seemed to resent the quite genuine enthusiasm of our tumultuous poetess.

> "*Arethusa arose, from her couch of snows,*
> *In the Acroceraunian mountains,*"

she was repeating to herself in a proud way, as she regarded the confined little lake, and the tall reeds, and the overhanging acacias.

"I don't see any mountains," he observed, pettishly.

"Of course not," she made answer, staring at him. "Acroceraunia is away over in Greece—in Epirus. Don't you know the story?"

His silence confessed his ignorance; and right eagerly—for it was a tale after her own heart—did she pour into his unwilling ear the legend of the passionate river-god and the flying maiden. But the Major was lying in wait for his revenge.

"She came all the way under the sea, and made her appearance here?" he asked.

"Yes, indeed," said the delighted Sappho. "They say that if you throw anything into the River Alpheus——"

"She was a goddess, I presume?" he asked again.

"Oh, yes; Arethusa was a daughter of Oceanus."

"I thought as much: if she came all the way under the Ionian Sea, she must have been an excellent Diva." And the wicked old man giggled and gurgled with laughter until he was purple in the face; and not only that, but he treasured up his wretched schoolboy witticism, so that every one on board the ship had heard of it before the evening. As for Sappho, she would pay no heed to such ribaldry. She gave Phaon's leading-string a twitch, and turned haughtily aside.

We weighed anchor about mid-day, and steamed slowly out of the harbour; and in due course of time we had lost sight of land again—nothing visible anywhere save that wide circle of trembling and shining blue, with a few motionless yellow-white clouds along the southern horizon. But although there was an abundance of leisure for everybody all the afternoon, it was not until the evening, in fact it was not until night fell, that Mrs. Threepenny-bit and her friend Peggy found an opportunity of talking over what had taken place on shore at Syracuse. They came right aft, to their accustomed corner behind the wheel-box, where there was little danger of their being overheard. And it soon became apparent that the elder woman had been much impressed by one or two circumstances that had come under her observation during the last day or two.

"I don't know what is going to happen," said she, rather sadly. "I have such a respect and liking for Mr. Wolfenberg—such an admiration for the simplicity and refinement of his character—yes, and such a sympathy for his lonely position——"

"And so have I," says Peggy, breaking in. "But when a married man allows himself to fall in love with an unmarried young woman he must take the consequences."

"Peggy!" the elder woman exclaims, indignantly. "That is not the situation at all. He is not in love with her, as a younger man might be. He has a great affection for her, no doubt, a most unselfish affection and care for her, every one can see that; and a deep interest in her and her future. I have told you all along that I considered the relationship existing between those two as a most beautiful thing—and I take her own description of it; but the difficulty is as to how any such relationship

can be made permanent. That is where the
danger comes in. He thinks, or he tries to
persuade himself, that her mind is too downright, her brain too clear, for her to give
way to the illusions of love ; she will never
marry ; her career is art ; she is an artist
through and through. So he seems to think.
But if she is an artist, she is also a woman."

"And very much of a woman," puts in
Peggy.

"Have you noticed how thoughtful and
careworn he has looked during the last day
or two ?" her companion goes on. "Do you
think he is beginning to see there is a possibility of Amélie Dumaresq falling away from
that compact—a possibility of his being left
alone ? Did you notice the expression of his
face yesterday, when he was standing by
himself away up there on the Greek Theatre,
and when she and the Russian had disappeared
below ? "

"A man cannot suffer the tortures of

jealousy unless he is in love," says Peggy,
in her frank way.

"It was something far wider and deeper
than that," says the other, absently. "It
appeared to me as if he were contemplating
the possible ruin—the second and final ruin
—of his life. All the schemes and hopes he
had been counting on for the future—all the
companionship and compensation he had been
promised—tumbling away from beneath his
feet: himself left betrayed by the very one
who had made a show of coming to his
rescue."

"Oh, no, no, Missis," says Peggy, with
some effort at cheerfulness; "it isn't so tragic
as all that—not yet, at all events. She has
been flirting with the Russian, no doubt;
and she may have had her head a little bit
turned. But you know the remarkably blunt
and plain things she says about marriage:
she is not likely to be entrapped. All this
will blow over; the Russian and his beautiful

eyes will disappear at the end of the voyage; and she will return to her loyal allegiance —to her art and her friend. Why, she is bound in honour! How often has she declared her determination to make up to him for what that other woman has done?"

Mrs. Threepenny-bit was silent for a long time.

"It seems such a piteous thing," she said at length, with a bit of a sigh, "that a man of his fine and sensitive character should be at the mercy of the caprice of any woman. But perhaps you are right, Peggy. Perhaps, after all, Amélie Dumaresq will recover her senses, and will remember what she undertook. We shall see—and that very soon, if I am not mistaken."

CHAPTER VIII.

"TO ATHENS SHALL THE LOVERS WEND."

WE are somewhere in the Ionian Sea. It is early morning, shining and calm. One happens to be alone on deck when a young man makes his appearance, and approaches. He is a youth of a diffident and ingenuous aspect—English-looking, with just enough of a moustache to lend excuse for a touch of pomatum. But when, after a great deal of apology, and blushing, and shy appealing of eyes, he blurts out what he wants, one finds his demand is not nearly so modest as his manner: he would like an introduction to Lady Cameron of Inverfask!

"The fact is," he goes on, in this nervous, embarrassed fashion, "I—I made the acquaintance of her sister Emily in Milan— and—I don't want to have anything under- hand about it——"

"Of course not; quite right. Why don't you go straight to Lady Cameron, and tell her you got to know her sister in Milan ?"

"It isn't as easy as all that," he answers, rather ruefully. "She might begin to question Emily—Miss Rosslyn, I mean. And—and— there was a kind of informality, don't you know. I suppose you heard of the lady Miss Rosslyn was travelling with being taken so seriously ill ; and her husband, Mr. Vincent, would not leave her for a moment almost ; and so—so, you see—Emily was pretty well alone. And I was staying in the same hotel. And—and she used to go every morning to the Cathedral—and then I used to meet her —and—and the Public Gardens are not far off. Well, perhaps I'd better tell you the downright truth at once. We are engaged to be married."

"The mischief you are!"

"At least, there is an understanding that is quite as good," he says; and then he goes on, with a little becoming hesitation: "And I don't see how any one can object. I am my own master now. I can make a settlement on Emily that I think will satisfy her family, however rich they may be——"

"They are not rich; they are poor—for Americans. But why on earth didn't you go to Lady Cameron the very moment you came on board at Palermo, and tell her the whole story?"

"It isn't as easy as you seem to think," he makes answer, almost in tones of reproach. "I'm in a kind of way under orders—from her. I've got to do as I'm bid. But she couldn't object to my writing home to my mother and sister: they are not in a position to ask questions. And, you see, if you would be so awfully kind as to introduce me to Lady Cameron, then through her I could make Emily's acquaintance all fair and square and above-board, in a proper and regular manner. That's how I am instructed, as the lawyers say," adds this poor young man, with a dolorous attempt at a smile.

" Very well ; come down early to lunch ; blunder into a seat at our table ; and then we'll see."

That, to our small circle, was the event of the day. Sharp at one the young man appeared at the door of the saloon ; he looked round with a pretty humility ; and at length came and gently subsided into the vacant seat opposite the Baby. A word or two introduced him to Lady Cameron, who was also on the other side of the table. And that was all he had bargained for ; indeed, formal introductions are rarely needed on board ship ; but how could one resist the temptation of confronting those two young wretches now that they were brought face to face ?

"Miss Emily, may I introduce to you Mr. Julian Verrinder?"

The two abandoned hypocrites bowed gravely: he, with downcast eyes, showing some little confusion; she, with her statuesque face grown pæony-like, not daring to look up. Yet perhaps their embarrassment remained unnoticed; for just at that moment Peggy, as a young house-mistress, was giving us her experiences of Highland servants as contrasted with the American (or sub-Irish) variety; and of course that was a most interesting topic for the other manager who rules over us all. But it seemed to one of us sitting there that a great and glorious nation like the Americans—a progressive nation—a nation clamorously calling attention to its gigantic strides—it seemed to one of us that such a nation should not stop short at the abolition of slavery; it should go a step further, and abolish domestic service altogether as degrading and inhuman.

" And who is to find work for all those people, then ? " said Mrs. Threepenny-bit. " Who is to support them ? "

" The State, of course ; State compensation."

" They are to be brought up in pampered idleness ? "

" Why, certainly ! "

" Then shall the valets rejoice and the maidservants skip like the young rams," observed Peggy, demurely—and fortunately she was but half-heard.

This was a hot and sultry and languorous afternoon. Peggy said she wished she had brought a few begging-letters with her, to hang up in her cabin ; their coolness, she imagined, would turn any place into a re-frigerator. Laziness was the order of the day on deck : books, chess, dominoes, draughts, surreptitious snoring. But of a sudden, just after sunset, a rumour ran like wild-fire through the ship that the coast of Greece was in sight ; there was a quick abandonment

of these various occupations, and a rush to
the rail; and there, sure enough, far away
in the north-east, beyond the dark indigo
sea, and half-hidden in a crimson-tinted mist
that caught its colour from the fading western
skies, rose one or two mountainous peaks,
pale and shadowy, in the neighbourhood of
Cape Matapan. At once our enthusiastic
Sappho was in a state of tremulous excitement. What was the ancient name of the
Cape? What?—Tænarium, where Hercules
slew the serpent? And Cape Malea was the
next point? And Cerigo—Cythera—was right
ahead of us? These other women—poor, vain,
soulless creatures—were now all going away
to their state-rooms to dress for dinner; but
not so Sappho; was it likely, when we
should soon be approaching the island where
Aphrodite sprang glorious from the white sea-
foam? The dusk fell. The sultry day had
been storing up electricity; blue lightning-
flashes began to play along the northern

horizon. But at length we also were forced to leave our good Sappho, her arms pensive on the rail; we guessed we should find some fruits of this rapt contemplation later on.

Now what vengeful god or goddess, what unholy witch or wizard, threw a spell of incantation over our ship on this succeeding night, so that during the dark hours we were whisked away some thousands of miles from our proper whereabouts? The next morning found us in the Sound of Sleat! There could be no doubt about it. A single glance out of the port-hole revealed the strangely familiar features—the calm, glassy blue sea; the bare, and lonely, and apparently tenantless islands; the first rays of the sun, streaming over from the east, lighting up those solitary shores. But—but—if this is the coast of Skye, where are the mighty Coolins with their black and jagged peaks piercing the heavens? And those islands, in their soft and beautiful rose-grey: are they not something warmer in

tone than the wind-swept Hebrides? And
then again, when one collects one's scattered
senses, ought we not by rights to be somewhere in the neighbourhood of Argolis, with
Hydra on the one hand, and Agio Giorgio
on the other, and before us the spacious Gulf
of Ægina? It is time to get on deck, to
clear up these bewildering doubts.

And here is Peggy, luckily all by herself.

"Do you know," she says, with something
of a rueful smile, "that when I got up this
morning and looked out, I thought I was
at home again!"—and when this tall young
lady talks about home, it is *not* Kentucky
she has in her mind, though 'twas there she
was born.

Suddenly she alters her tone.

"Now that we have a minute together,"
says she, rather indignantly, "perhaps you
will tell me when I am to get back to my
own friends. I came away with you. I did

not bargain to go about with an inspired maniac of a poetess and a swearing old Major making bad jokes——"

"Oh, oh! For you to say anything against the Major—considering his devotion to you—and the way you have been openly carrying-on with him——"

"Carrying on!" she says. "Much chance of carrying on with anybody—while the Baby's great eyes are staring at you all the time!"

"Perhaps the Baby might as well look to herself," one ventures to say.

"What do you mean?"

"Oh, nothing. But here is some information for you. You know it was merely because we had Amélie Dumaresq thrown on our hands that you and we got separated when we went on shore. But this time, while we are at Athens, the Dumaresqs are going to stay at an hotel, to save the trouble of coming back each night to the steamer. And you may be sure that the Major will dine at an hotel, for the sake of variety—yes, and Sappho, too, if anybody will ask her——"

"And we shall be together again and by ourselves!" says Peggy, with a quick delight shining in her eyes. "That will be something to make up! And I'll tell you what we must do. After dinner the Missis and you must come into my cabin; and I'll get out my banjo; and we'll have one of the real old evenings! I think we'll give old Father Time what for; we'll make things hum a little!" But here her face falls. "There's the Baby—I forgot her."

"Is she so very austere?"

"Oh, she is too solemn for anything!" says Peggy, with a certain impatience, though she is fond enough of the serious-minded Emily all the same. "She ought to go into some religious retreat—some sisterhood: that will be the end of it all, I know. And here she is coming now. Didn't I tell you? I never can get a word with anybody, without finding her big eyes staring at me ! "

And so we steamed on through the luminous and glancing azure, on the one hand the ruddy island of Ægina, on the other the mountainous coast that leads away down to "Sunium's marbled steep." It was a delightful, idle, dreamy kind of morning— not the kind of morning on which one wanted to be startled or even surprised; so that when a very gentle-voiced and gentle-eyed lady came up to our Mrs. Threepenny-bit, and held out her binocular glass, and said quietly—

"Wouldn't you like to look at the Acropolis ? "—the smaller woman could only stammer out, in a frightened sort of way :

"The—the Acropolis of Athens ? "

The next instant she was on her feet, staring eagerly and goggle-eyed. For yonder, unmistakably, were the distant and lofty heights, with a glimmer of grey columns, and with a strip of grey town far below; and yonder, too, were the scarred and shaggy slopes of Mount Hymettus; while down by the blue sea was the bold scimitar-sweep of the shores of Salamis. The first impression we received was one of extreme loneliness and lifelessness, despite the presence of that powdered grey city. There was not a boat moving anywhere on these shining clear waters; the coast-line seemed strangely un-inhabited. For one thing, we were not going round into the Peiræus, on account of certain rumours of fever that had reached us at Syracuse; we were making in for the solitary little Bay of Phalerum; and that we took possession of, and had all to ourselves.

"Peggy," said Mrs. Threepenny-bit, some little time thereafter, when we had got ready to go ashore for a preliminary look round—and she spoke in a low voice—"have you heard? Mr. Hitrovo is going to stay at the same hotel with the Dumarescqs."

Peggy said nothing, but looked much.

"And they have asked us to lunch with them to-morrow," her friend continued; "and I have accepted, for all of us."

"Will the Russian be there?" asked Peggy.

"That depends on whether Amélie Dumaresq wants him to be there. It is all her arrangement. If she wishes him to be there he will be there. She has a way of getting everything she wants—even if it were the moon, I should think."

"And Wolfenberg?"

"Peggy," said the smaller woman, "Mr. Wolfenberg is in charge of them! Do you mean to say there might be a possibility of the Russian being present as their guest—making up a family party, almost—and Wolfenberg absent? That would be too—too—much!"

"Yet such things have happened," observed Peggy, calmly, as she watched the men bringing the boats round to take us in to the land.

Truly it is an ignominious thing that you

have to approach Athens by either rail or
tramway; but travellers must be content; and
when we got ashore we took our tickets in the
empty little station of Phalerum, just as if we
had been going to Greenwich. And when the
train came in, our party of four got possession
of a compartment in the most ordinary way :
there positively would have been no enthusiasm, no excitement, no recalling of ancient
deeds and ancient glories, had not our dear
Sappho skipped in also, followed by the
Major in pursuit of Peggy. And in vain
did Sappho strive to conceal her exaltation.
As we moved out into the arid and dusty
plain, she was all eagerness to catch a glimpse
of the River Cephissus—the Cephissus in
which the youthful Theseus had bathed before
going to the palace of King Ægeus to claim
his rights. Alas ! there was no Cephissus.
It had all gone away. We saw one or two
channels in the limy soil that might at one
time or another have been a river-bed; but

were now more likely to be frequented by lizards than by fish. And there would be no Ilissus either, then? she demanded. And no Fountain of Callirrhoe?

"The whole place is burned up," said the Major, who seemed secretly to rejoice in her disappointment. "And shan't we be roasted alive in this blessed town! I tell you, about the only cool thing we are likely to find in Athens is the frieze of the Parthenon."

He giggled; but no one else did. This brutality seemed to set the seal on our degradation. It was only fit that we should arrive in Athens carrying railway-tickets in our hands.

But on reaching the terminus we managed to throw off those two: our party of four just filled a carriage; and, as we drove away, we caught sight of the Major having perforce, and probably with a very ill grace, to offer a seat in his vehicle to his forlorn companion. We saw no more of Sappho for a long time thereafter—not, indeed, until we found her in front of the little Temple of Nike Apteros, absorbed and awe-stricken, and no doubt dreaming of the black-sailed ships coming back from Crete, far out on yonder blue plain of sea.

We made direct away for the Acropolis, of course ; our first stage in the ever-ascending route being the Temple of Theséus, where we found the Dumaresqs and Wolfenberg—the Russian being unexpectedly absent. Amélie Dumaresq—who was somehow always the central figure of any such chance-formed group, and whose opinions seemed to demand attention—did not appear to have been impressed by the Theseum. It was smaller than she had anticipated. It had been copied so often that itself looked like a copy. Roofed over, it had the appearance of a museum. It was too complete. There was not enough ruin about it. If the Venetians, in besieging the Acropolis, had thrown a few bombs into this building, and knocked it about a bit, it would have been infinitely improved. It wanted the letting in of daylight—and a background of blue sky for the pillars. And so forth. Wolfenberg listened.

"Amélie," said he, with a smile, "come with me. I will show you something that will interest you."

He took her to the end of the building where, out of range of the sunlight, there were several swarthy-complexioned figures lying in various attitudes prone on the steps, either asleep or merely basking in luxurious idleness. It was all very picturesque and fine in colour: the diverse costumes, the warm tones of the shadowed marble, the palpitating, hot air beyond, the aerial tints of the distant hills. And here, also, walking about in very brave array, were a couple of Cretans—a couple of unmistakable cut-throats, if physiognomy ever spoke a word of truth. They stared at her; she stared at them; it was not her eyes—

those bold, lustrous black eyes—that were first abashed.

But then again, when our panting horses had dragged us away up the stony hill, and when on foot we had ascended the worn and steep steps of the Propylæa, and when at length, after toiling across a wilderness of broken pillars, pedestals, architraves, cornices, and the like, the marble fragments lying tumbled about among parched weeds and thistles—when at length we came in front of the Parthenon, there was no disposition to criticise, nor even to speak, manifested by this young woman. Such artist-soul as she possessed seemed entirely entranced by the simplicity and grandeur of this spectacle; and not only that, but by the actual beauty of the colour—those lonely and lofty columns, golden-white and saffron-stained, shining calm and fair against the dark, deep, pellucid-blue of a perfectly cloudless sky. No picture or any other representation of the Parthenon,

can give any one the faintest idea of this
rich and vivid and exquisite colour; nor can
all the photographs that ever were manu-
factured convey the least impression of the
vastness of the ruin, or of its height, and
remoteness from the rest of the surrounding
world. You forget that there is a populous
city with its swarms of houses lying scattered
about somewhere down in the valley. You
forget the long centuries of wrong and rapine
and outrage that have swept by like so many
tempests, destroying much, but not destroying all. These columns, broken and defaced
as they are, seem to rise above such transitory
things—to be somehow dissociated from the
earth; voiceless, they appear to be holding
communion with the still heavens; and to
have become immortal through their imperish-
able beauty. For already we had begun to
yield to the strange fascination that, while
you are in Athens, seems to draw you
involuntarily away up to this grand, lonely,

beautiful thing, and to leave you pretty well indifferent to aught else.

Not but that there were plenty of other objects of intensest interest, up here on the Acropolis. Each one of our scattered party seemed to go his own way, wandering about, finding out for himself or herself, and not anxious for any companionship. Groups formed by accident; then separated again; one amateur explorer would be chiefly interested in the traces left by Turk and Christian on the Greek walls; another would go about examining the ornamentation of fallen pediments and capitals; a third might have his eyes attracted by the great panorama of sea, and plain, and mountain, with the marble quarries of Pentelicus gleaming white on the far hill-side. And so it was without any surprise that one came across Ernest Wolfenberg, standing quite by himself, in front of the little Temple of the Caryatides.

" Isn't it strange," he began to say, in his

thoughtful and dispassionate manner, "how difficult it is for the official mind—and for some other minds as well—to draw the line between preservation and restoration ? They cannot for the life of them leave things alone ; they must of necessity bring in the modern mechanic to tinker and beautify. And there's another thing they can't resist doing : when they find anything detachable they can't help rushing off with it at once to a museum, and putting it in a glass case if that is possible. And yet half the value of memorials of ancient life and art lies in their being allowed to remain *in situ*. Just imagine how immeasurably interesting it would be if the excavators would leave a house in Pompeii precisely as they found it : every object— every knitting-needle, and lamp, and dish, and wine-glass—in its place, just as it was when the ashes began to fall. But they couldn't bring themselves to do that. They must snatch up every article, and away with

it to the Naples Museum, where there are
dozens and hundreds of them already. And
the restorers are infinitely worse. Look at
this beautiful little building that has been
talked about for ages and ages. I suppose
putting in that wedge of entablature may be
forgiven—perhaps it was necessary ; but, you
see, they couldn't stop there ; they had to add
a brand new Caryatid. The Temple of the
Six Virgins ought to have six figures ; they
couldn't leave it with five ; so they added a
new one. And then, naturally, you begin
to consider everything suspect. These bits
of egg-and-dart decoration lying about : how
do you know that the modern mechanic's
chisel has not been tinkering at them ? And
yet," he went on presently, "I must try to
believe that the scroll-work inside the
Erectheum has been left untouched : it is
so indescribably beautiful. Did you notice
it particularly in the inner temple and over
the doorway ? It is well sheltered there ;

perhaps that accounts for its perfect state. Come, shall we go round and have another look ? "

Well, a second visit, although the afternoon was drawing on, was no great hardship; for the Erectheum is far and away the most graceful of all the Acropolis monuments. Moreover, the entrance was only a few yards distant. But we were suddenly to be recalled from these architectural questions to more living interests. We were just about to pass round by the steps leading up to the tall and elegant Ionic pillars, when we perceived two figures there, at the base of the columns, and perhaps half a yard or so within. They were Paul Hitrovo and Amélie Dumaresq. It could not be said that there was any effort at concealment on their part; still, their appearance here was in a measure startling; for the Russian had not hitherto been visible during the day. Another thing: ordinarily, in talking to Hitrovo, Amélie regarded him with frank and upturned and smiling eyes ; but now her head was downcast ; her face was concerned and grave ; she was vaguely scoring the dust with the point of her sunshade. IIe, on the other hand, had his eyes intently fixed on her—so that neither noticed the approach of strangers.

Wolfenberg turned quickly aside—perhaps pretending to have seen nothing.

"Some other time—any time—" he said, hurriedly, and yet with some affectation of calm indifference. "The fact is, a preliminary glance round is quite enough for to-day ; now we know where to come for closer study. And —and we must not let the women-folk get tired, especially Mrs. Dumaresq, who is not very strong. Have you seen her of late ? I suppose she is sitting down somewhere, talking to some one. I must go and try to find her anyway. There are your people coming round yonder by the Parthenon." And so he went away ; and those two, whatever they were talking about, were left undisturbed.

It was drawing towards dusk when we got back to the little wooden jetty at Phalerum; and twilight had fallen by the time the ship's boat had carried us out to the *Orotania.* This evening, at dinner, we had a new experience : the vacant spaces at our table were conspicuous. And we should hardly have imagined that we should so have felt the absence of three people who, not so very long ago, had been entirely strangers to us. But there was this about Amélie Dumaresq in particular—that whether she attracted or repelled you, you could not but be impressed by her presence. She was there, very much in evidence; of strong and assertive vitality; full-pulsating, as it were, with gaiety and the enjoyment of life; and perfectly well aware of all her wilfulness, her charm, her intrepid opinions, and (not least) the power of the laughing blaze of her black eyes. Wolfenberg, too, in his more retiring way, had grown to interest us deeply; we seemed to miss the fine, thoughtful, ascetic face, the sympathetic grey eyes, even the quietly humorous fashion in which he was wont to apologise for the young lady's audacities. As for the sad-faced mother—-But she was content to remain mostly in the background, a not unconcerned spectator of what was going on.

However, we were not wholly deserted; for Julian Verrinder, seeing these unoccupied places, made bold to come and take one of them, with many and modest excuses. And nothing could exceed the courteous and pleasant manner in which he tried to ingratiate himself with Lady Cameron and with our Mrs. Threepenny-bit, offering them all kinds of things they didn't want, asking them shy questions about their day's doings, and meekly listening, and never obtruding a word about himself. And he agreed with all their opinions, before they had got them half uttered; until they could not but have been convinced that he was a most intelligent

young man. On the surface he did not pay
much attention to Emily Rosslyn; but he
had the ineffable pleasure of tendering her the
cruet-stand, in the temporary absence of the
steward, or he would venture to recommend
the fresh salad, or the olives, or the caviare.
As for her, the young wretch affected to treat
him as almost an absolute stranger; she would
hardly even vouchsafe him a timid "No,
thank you!" Perhaps she was in trembling
terror lest some incautious word or sign might
betray the amazing truth.

It was a beautiful night on deck, the stars
and planets lambent in the deep violet vault.
There was a perfect silence: the famous city
was far enough away to send us no sound,
while we guessed that now there would not
be much of tumult up there on the solitary
heights of the Acropolis, near to the throbbing
and yet benign and tranquil skies. If there
could be anything anywhere out of consonance
with the prevailing calm in which the world

was shrouded, it could only be, perhaps, in some solitary and aching heart, questioning itself, or nerving itself for the future ; and such things are kept hidden away and unrevealed.

"Did you speak to Mr. Wolfenberg to-day ?" asked Peggy of her friend, as they were leaning on the rail, and looking across the black water to the dim, uncertain lights.

"Oh yes."

"And he is to be of the party at the hotel to-morrow ?"

"I understand so."

"I am glad of that," she says ; and then she adds, slowly : "Because—because—otherwise, I don't think I should have gone."

CHAPTER IX.

FACING CONTINGENCIES.

THE gods were good to Sappho on the following day: they called the lost Ilissus back to life again: Cephissus, also, they summoned from his subterranean lair. We had been driving about hither and thither during the morning —to a number of places it is needless to enumerate here; and all the while we had been conscious of an ever-increasing darkness overhead. Indeed it was welcome; for we had become tired of that long period of blue skies, blue seas, and glaring sunlight; and were quite glad to think of the coolness of a shower of rain. But there was more coming than we bargained for. The surrounding mountains had grown more and more sombre;

they seemed to draw strangely near, as if they would hem in the doomed town ; the air was stifling ; the impending darkness deepened, and still further deepened ; what wan light there was came in horizontally, and touched the fronts of the houses in a spectral fashion. Then, as we watched and waited in this ominous silence, of a sudden, out of the black bosom of the hills, there leapt a red flash of flame ; it struck down ; it appeared to splinter itself on the ground, and to spread itself out again in swift and trembling filaments of fire. There was a low premonitory growl—answered somewhere else. Another blaze of flame leapt out of the black : this time there was a sharper rattle, that echoed all around. And now the fun grew fast and furious ; the other portions of the heavens joined in ; sometimes there was a continuous and blinding dazzle of crimson— a chain of fire, as it were ; while the noise grew deafening—Corydallus, Pentelicus, Hymettus calling to each other across the awe-stricken valleys. Then the accumulated black masses immediately over us must needs take part; there were one or two knife-like gleams of pink; and at the same moment an ear-splitting roar and clamour that seemed to say that all the buildings of the Acropolis—the Parthenon, the Propylæa, the Erectheum—were coming hurling headlong down on the top of the devoted city. And meanwhile the rain had been descending in sheets—a deluge that appeared to consist of ten thousand waterspouts; insomuch that in an incredibly short space of time Athens had become completely transfigured, her dry and dusty thoroughfares changed into tawny canals, with a flood in them so deep and opaque that the unaccustomed horses refused to go forward. As for ourselves, we fled for refuge into the nearest public building, which chanced to be the museum in which the Schliemann relics (from Mycenæ) are treasured; but even here we had to face cascades of water that came surging along the open stone galleries and down the wide staircases. But what did we care for all this terrific commotion—and also for having to wade a foot deep in passing from one room to the other—when we could calculate on this amazing storm having roused the two slumbering rivers, and, when we thought of the joy and rapture of our beloved Sappho ? For we knew that, as we went back to Phalerum in the afternoon, we should find the Cephissus a whirling and riotous torrent, sweeping before it mud, and gravel, and branches onwards to the sea, and also that the wide plain which had always seemed to us so parched and burnt-up would now show silver-glancing pools and lakes, between the rows of olive and vine. Perhaps, moreover, in some happy moment, we might discover the elusive Fountain of Callirrhoe, that hitherto had been for us invisible.

But in the meantime we had to keep our appointment with the Dumaresqs ; and when, at length, after about two hours' imprisonment in this building, a pale, tremulous, lemon-hued light told us that the storm-clouds were lifting themselves away from the deluged city, we ventured out, and drove away down through those yellow canals to the hotel. And here, in the long, bare, shaded, foreign-looking apartment, it was from the outset obvious that it was Amélie Dumaresq, not her mother, who was our hostess. She managed everything—arranged everything—consulted with the landlord—directed the waiters. She was in high spirits; this little diversion from the routine life on board ship seemed to please her. She was looking her best, too; and was very prettily and neatly attired, with but little ornament; a dagger of rose-red coral was effective in the splendid masses of her black hair.

She took the head of the table as a matter of course—to save her mother trouble. Wolfenberg she asked to preside at the other end. To Paul Hitrovo she did *not* give the place of honour on her right ; his presence there was significant enough without that ; and, in truth, she affected to take but scant notice of him. As for him, he remained carelessly quiet throughout the little banquet ; he did not seek to interfere in the conversation ; when he did speak at all, it was generally some mere bit of comment—of a half-cynical and not unamusing kind. He was next to the Baby. "The two young people must sit together," Amélie Dumaresq had said, benignly—playing the part of matron and house-mistress.

And now that everything was set going, the young hostess proceeded with right good will to entertain her guests, which for her was easy enough. Laughing, chattering, appealing to this one and that, revealing the results of a rather malicious observation of her fellow-passengers, she kept the ball of conversation rolling briskly enough and without effort, so alert, independent, many-sided did she show herself. And again on this occasion she was merciful to us. She did not hack and hew at the pedestals of accepted tradition; she did not tear down veils to exhibit shattered idols; she even let Homer alone — and was entirely good-natured. If there was any one whose speeches did not seem to meet with the full approval of our miniature Censor of Morals it was M. Paul Hitrovo; and yet such chance things as we heard were surely harmless enough.

"Isn't it sad," he said, in a kind of under tone, to the Baby, *àpropos* of something or another, "isn't it very sad to think of the vast number of people who are slaves to duty? It seems such a strange superstition."

Well, that was nothing. But on one occasion he did manage to provoke our Mrs. Threepenny-bit into a little mild interference.

"After all," he happened to say to that ingenuous young neighbour of his, "human nature is a good deal stronger than the Ten Commandments."

"You mean that sometimes the Ten Commandments get broken?" the small woman opposite him put in.

"Why not say frequently?" he suggested, with a smile.

"Perhaps," she answered him. "But at the same time, if there never had been any Mount Sinai at all, human nature would have had to invent the Ten Commandments for its own preservation."

It was hardly a rebuke; yet Amélie Dumaresq looked quickly from the one to the other; perhaps she was anxious to see what impression this young man, in these more intimate circumstances, produced on her friends.

To outward appearance she was far more attentive to Wolfenberg. She paid him all kinds of little flatteries—sometimes disguised as reproach.

"Ernest," she called to him, "don't you see that the very heavens are interposing to befriend you? This miracle of a flood has all come about to show you the Fountain of Callirrhoe. You can have no further excuse for neglecting your picture. Why, I want those people on board the ship who have never seen any of your work just to understand a little who it is to whom they say 'Good morning!' when they come up on deck."

"I'm afraid, Amélie," he said, in his quiet way, "the Fountain of Callirrhoe has all gone away—vanished—as far as I am concerned. I have not thought of it of late. It was only a passing suggestion."

"Well, if you have lost interest in it, why not begin something else?" she demanded, in her downright fashion. ". Why not the Dance of the Cobras? Do you know," she said, turning to her other guests, "that cobras have the strangest habit, on moonlight nights, of keeping their head erect, and swaying themselves from side to side, and watching their shadows on the ground? They seem to enjoy it; the sinuous movement pleases them. Don't you think that Mr. Wolfenberg could make something very mysterious and imaginative out of such a subject? And they are said to be curiously susceptible to musical sound, too. Couldn't that be brought in?— a verandah—some one playing inside—the beasts charmed out from their hiding-places into the moonlight—— "

" It makes one's flesh creep to think of it!" said Mrs. Threepenny-bit, with an involuntary shudder.

" Oh, I like looking into the snake-cases in the Zoological Gardens," said Amélie Dumaresq, cheerfully enough. " But what I confess I cannot do is to look into the monkey-house. That is quite different. Any other beast I can stare in the face—but a monkey—no— I somehow feel ashamed. It seems as if I were guilty of impertinence—as if I had shut up a poor relation in there—and might at least pass on and pretend not to see. Don't his eyes reproach you? He appears to ask why he should be so treated—why he should be put behind bars, just like an ordinary wild beast; while you are walking about at liberty, in splendid silks and satins. But Ernest—come, now—what about the cobras in moonlight? I really cannot have those people talking to you as if you were one of themselves; they must know who you are; I must have something to show them——"

"My dear Amélie," he said, quite good-naturedly, "what is the use of painting nowadays? Picture-buying is a lost art——"

"Oh, for you to say that!" she exclaimed, in reproachful tones.

"The fact is," he said, "I am going to take to another way of earning my living altogether. Shall I tell you? Very well. I don't know whether you are aware that only sixty-seven eggs of the great auk are known to exist. Of course they are extremely valuable. One of them was recently sold for three hundred pounds. Now I propose to introduce on the scene an ancient and simple sea-captain—a whaler or sealer from Baffin's Bay, or some such remote place ; and he must have a circumstantial story of a discovered island, where he found a heap of big eggs, which he brought home out of mere curiosity. He doesn't know that they are the great auk's eggs ; of course not ; but still, the simple mariner won't accept the first bid for them—— "

" But where can he have got them, if they are so rare ? " she interposed.

" I am going to make them for him," he replied, calmly. " An imitation that will defy detection—far more easy than you think. Besides, the honest tar's story would ward off suspicion. No doubt the price of auk's eggs will come down somewhat ; but even at 150*l*. a piece, or even at 100*l*. a piece, a good steady supply—from the inexhaustible stores of the sealer's cabin—ought to make one's fortune."

"Well, well, Ernest!" she said. "And you are not ashamed to sit there and confess, before English people, that the tradition of wooden nutmegs still lingers in the American national character?"

But all the same his fantastic fancy of the moment had served its end: it had drawn away the talk from the question of his painting; and we had noticed ere now that he was curiously shy about having his work spoken of before strangers. Amélie Dumaresq did not seem to understand, or at least to pay much heed to, this sensitiveness; and in the present case it was of slight consequence; for directly she was off and away to some other topic, with her usual happy-go-lucky impetuosity. It was a merry little occasion, free and unrestrained, as one might have thought, with nothing serious at all about it. But women's eyes are always observant.

That same night, when Peggy and her friend had secured a snug corner for themselves on deck—the heavens were all clear again, and the stars were throbbing luminously over the dark spaces of the sea—you may be sure it was to that midday festivity that their conversation turned.

"I tell you, Missis, I am convinced of it,' says Peggy, with as much decision as she dare put into her necessarily low tones. "I tell you that man is in love with her, wholly, entirely, desperately in love with her—whether he himself knows it or not."

"What, the Russian?"

"Not at all! The Russian is only playing with her. He is too much in love with himself to be in love with anybody else. He thinks he has only got to look at you with his beautiful eyes, and you must succumb. He does not take the trouble to make himself agreeable; he expects you to amuse him; and then he

smiles—and you are rewarded! No—it is
Wolfenberg——

"You are speaking of a married man,
Peggy!" the other observes, severely.

"Worse luck," says Peggy, with a bit of
a sigh. "But whether he himself knows it
or not, that man is in love with Amélie
Dumaresq; and this understanding of theirs
—this compact—this exalted friendship—is
with him only some desperate clinging on to
what he feels must one day slip away from
him. In love with her? Didn't you see how
his eyes followed her wherever she went—as
if it was a constant delight to him to let them
rest even on the folds of her dress, or the
coils of her hair, or the outline of her neck
and arms. He speaks to her as he speaks
to no one else. His voice changes when he
turns to her—it is so gentle, so intimate, so
suggestive of an understanding that is hidden
from outsiders. Perhaps she doesn't quite
perceive it either. She is a little blunt—

don't you think?—not exactly thick-skinned
—but—but pretty well wrapped up in herself,
and her own enjoyment of minute to minute?
Of course, she has an immense admiration for
him; but it seems to me as if it were more
the artist she admired; she is proud of his
position, and his advice, and his care of her,
as well she might be."

"But what is to come of it all!" the elder
woman exclaims—and this is no new cry of
hers. "Oh, I cannot believe it! The position
those two hold to each other is far too clearly
defined for any such possibility; in her mind,
at all events, it is defined clearly and
absolutely; hasn't she talked about it with
sufficient frankness? No; really I thought
there was something almost noble about her
when she first spoke to me about it; she
seemed to see what was demanded of her;
she seemed to rise to something finer than
the gratification of her own immediate whims,
and the flattery of every one who comes near

her. And why shouldn't he take her at her word? He declares that her intellect is downright and uncompromising; she scorns illusions; this exalted companionship of theirs, when she grants it to him, is granted with full and accurate knowledge; there are no hazy possibilities of perilous sentiment hanging about in the background. Do you think he does not understand all that?"

"I can see what his eyes say," Peggy makes answer, stubbornly. "Until to-day I might have doubted—now I cannot."

But the elder woman shakes her head.

"No, no; the whole situation is dangerous enough without that. And it is about Wolfenberg that I am concerned: I think the young woman can take care of herself. And yet again if it should turn out that we have been speculating, and alarming ourselves without cause—or if something were to happen—— "

"I know what would happen in a book or

a play," says Peggy. "That dreadful woman over there in America would die. But in actual life the objectionable people are a long time in dying; and in the meanwhile the other people, who may have been waiting, have grown old."

"You have no right to look forward and count on anyone's death!" says Mrs. Three-penny-bit, with a touch of asperity. "It is inhuman—unnatural—no matter what has happened." And then, after a bit, she adds: "Don't you think, Peggy, that it would be a little more just to both Wolfenberg and Amélie Dumaresq if we accepted their own account of the relationship that exists between them—which is the only relationship that can exist between them?"

"But even then?" says Peggy. "Again and again you yourself have put the question: what guarantee is there that such a relation-ship should last? What is the bond between them? It is an ideal situation, no doubt;

demanding self-sacrifice and constancy; and it may look beautiful at the moment; but what safeguard is there against all the temptations and incomprehensible vagaries of human nature?"

"Poor Wolfenberg!" said the elder woman, absently; the future seemed dark and enigmatical enough to her, so far as those two were concerned.

Now the morning of our last day at Athens was particularly bright, and busy, and cheerful. "Phaleron's wave" is clear: looking over the side into those green deeps, we could vaguely make out objects at the bottom, though we were anchored in six fathoms of water; while farther off the glassy surface, in the full glare of the sun, reflected the long lateen sails and the white-painted feluccas with a vividness bewildering to the eyes. And here was our indefatigable Sappho, bustling about with a great sheet of paper in her hand, and eagerly begging for signatures. It appeared that her soul had been fairly riven within her by the thought that English hands had harried the shrines of ancient Greece; and nothing would do but a passionate appeal, on the part of us Orotanians, to the British Government, praying that the Elgin marbles should forthwith be restored. It was an eloquent and tempestu- ously-worded document, with plenty of in- coherent indignation surging through it; and at the head of the sheet was the following quotation :

' Cold is the heart, fair Greece ! that looks on thee,
Nor feels as lovers o'er the dust they loved ;
Dull is the eye that will not weep to see
Thy walls defaced, thy mouldering shrines removed
By British hands, which it had best behoved
To guard those relics ne'er to be restored.
Curst be the hour when from their isle they roved,
And once again thy hapless bosom gored,
And snatch'd thy shrinking Gods to northern climes
    abhorr'd ! '

"Somethinged sentimental rubbish!" growled the angry Major, when she had gone—and we hardly knew whether he was audaciously referring to the passage from *Childe Harold* or merely expressing his opinion of Miss Penguin's proposal. "Do you think the English Government would listen to a handful of irresponsible and impertinent busybodies? And if these mongrel modern Greeks got back the Elgin Marbles, what would they do with 'em? Why, sell 'em to some Yankee hotel proprietor, to stick about his staircases, alongside the cuspidors!"

By the way, we never learned what number of signatures Sappho obtained for her petition; nor did we ever subsequently hear of its having appeared in the newspapers. Perhaps, indeed, at some odd moment, Phaon may have eaten it, so inscrutable are the decrees of fate and the moods of a dog's appetite.

Our last day at Athens. Of course, we made our way back again to the Acropolis. And as we were toiling up the steep hill we chanced to notice the solitary figure of a man who was coming down from the scarred and bouldered heights of Areopagus. No doubt he had wandered up thither to have a look at the wide-scattered city lying far below, with its red-tiled roofs and cypress-gardens.

" It is Wolfenberg ! " said Mrs. Threepenny-bit, with some surprise. " And alone ! Why —surely, the others cannot have gone any-where without him." And when she spoke of " the others " we knew she was thinking of three.

" Oh, no, impossible ! " said Peggy, in an undertone, for now he was drawing near.

But when he came up, we found he had no tragic tale of desertion to tell. He seemed in fairly good spirits. Mrs. Dumaresq had pre-ferred to remain indoors this morning ; she feared the heat ; and she wanted a little rest. Nor did Amélie care to stir out. She had been making some purchases of millinery ; and wished to get her things put in order before returning to the boat. So he had come wandering away by himself, counting on finding us somewhere about the Acropolis. Accordingly, we went on together.

But when we had got up to that lofty and spacious plateau, to have a farewell look at the hills and the vales, the distant sea grown pale in the sunlight, and here, close at hand, the splendour of the tall pillars against the luminous blue of the sky, it very soon became obvious that Wolfenberg wished to take this opportunity to say something in confidence to the elder woman of our little group. They strolled away by themselves, and Peggy instinctively hung back. We saw them go slowly and still more slowly, apparently engaged in earnest conversation, until they stopped together—the two small figures out yonder on the plain of tumbled fragments and dusty weeds. Peggy was silent for a second or two ; then she said—

" I think he means to speak to her about the Russian. And I am glad of it. He ought to have some confidante. Don't you think he is in the strangest and saddest position ? Mrs. Dumaresq is frightened to say anything to him about what has happened recently : no wonder. She is quite useless and helpless with an absolute and self-willed girl like that; and she is mortally afraid of doing or saying anything that may offend either Wolfenberg or her daughter." She glanced round her musingly. " Isn't it curious to think what various things have happened to individual human beings, up here on this hill, through all the centuries since those stones were carved ? And now we have come to the very latest—the two people over yonder, in modern European dress, standing talking to each other. It seems commonplace, doesn't it ; and yet it might turn out to be something tragic enough——" She suddenly broke off, and changed her tone. " No, no, I'm going to shut my eyes, and become optimist. I'm going to look forward to Amélie Dumaresq herself dispersing away all these doubts and fears. That is what she is going to do. The opportunity is before her. She is going to astonish us, and charm us, and make us all ashamed of ourselves, by showing herself nothing less than a thorough heroine!"

Meanwhile, whatever problem of human destiny or human character those two were discussing together, they were a long time engaged in it; so that the rest of us—including the Baby and Julian Verrinder, whose acquaintance with each other seemed to have developed with some rapidity—had abundant leisure for our final look round; and at length, when we all of us prepared to leave, Peggy's last word—as she glanced back to the beautiful temples all shattered and ruined—was this—

"Well, Athens did much for the Gods; but the Gods never seem to have done much for Athens."

Now hardly had the *Orotania* got under weigh again when two of us received a summons to go to Mrs. Threepenny-bit's cabin. The little woman appeared to be rather nervous and excited : it was clear she had something of importance to communicate.

" We had a long talk up there," she said (and well we knew of whom she was speaking), " and never shall I forget it as long as I live. I had some admiration for that man before ; but now—now that he has quite revealed himself—I dare hardly say what I think of him. And there is no secret about it ; he spoke quite frankly ; he told me, in his simple and direct way, that we must all of us have seen the favour that Amélie was showing to this young Russian ; and he hoped it would turn out for the best. It was but natural, he said. She was a young woman, with a fresh and eager and impulsive enjoyment of the world and all its interests : who could wonder if the passion of love came in to play its part, and lead on to marriage, and a happy settlement of her life ? And when I interposed, and spoke of himself, I wish you could have heard what he answered. Not that I forget a single word; but that there was something so noble, so simple, so unreserved in the very manner in which he put himself out of the question altogether. He was not to be thought of. His was a broken life altogether, he said. If this new interest that appeared to have come into her existence was likely to secure her happiness, that was everything."

The person who was telling us these things is not of a very emotional nature; but, all the same, her lashes grew moist; and she furtively drew a finger-tip across her eyes.

"I thought his careworn face looked really beautiful as he was speaking," she went on, with an intensity of sympathy that caused her own voice to vibrate at times. "There seemed to me a kind of sanctity of renunciation in it; and a calmness, too, as though he had been contemplating this possibility not for the first time. He would hardly refer to himself at all. I had to do that. I confess I am a good deal more concerned about him than about her. But what he said was this: 'I put myself aside altogether. I had indulged a foolish dream : it must go, if there is need for it to go. Why not ? What man has borne, man can bear ; a sharp pang or two, and life grown a little greyer ; but the years will go by all the same.' And again he said—but I wish you could have seen the strange expression of his face, in its calm heroism of resignation : he said—'What right had I to think that a beautiful young creature like that, full of life and the enjoyment of life, should check the natural current of her existence—even for the sake of her art ? I was wrong even there. If she must give up her work ; if marriage is the one thing to secure her happiness—so be it. But at all events do not think that she has broken any understanding, or betrayed any- body, or done anything but what is perfectly right and straightforward and honest. *She* knows what I care most for—it is to see her perfectly happy : that being secured, my small affairs can shift for themselves.' "

" And about Hitrovo ? " Peggy asked.

" Yes, that was his chief anxiety, his sole anxiety," her friend continued. " And I told him frankly that Mrs. Dumaresq had spoken to us ; and that she was very much concerned ; and that we had promised to make inquiries at Constantinople. But do not imagine it was to provoke suspicion, or to ask me to caution Amélie, that Wolfenberg came to me. Quite the reverse. He had nothing but commendation for the young Russian. He said it was so natural that Amélie should be attracted by him—his singularly good looks—his pleasant manner—his desire to please——"

" Oh, if he takes it in that way, I am so glad," Peggy exclaimed, quite effusively. " I had been fearing such terrible things. I pitied him so ! "

" Peggy," said the smaller woman, " Ernest Wolfenberg has not got that firm mouth for nothing. Do you think he cannot bring himself to face the inevitable—if it should turn out to be the inevitable? And of one thing you may be sure: Amélie Dumaresq will never know, she will never be allowed to know, what is going on in that man's heart, so long as he sees her happy, and beloved, and content." She paused for a moment or two; then she said—" Well, that poor woman, Mrs. Dumaresq, has made a direct appeal to us. Perhaps we may hear something in Constantinople."

And so, as the evening came along, we made our way down towards Cape Colonna; and then the dusk fell; and the dark; and thereafter we went thundering onwards through the night.

END OF VOL. I.

LONDON: PRINTED BY WILLIAM CLOWES AND SONS, LIMITED,
STAMFORD STREET AND CHARING CROSS.

www.ingramcontent.com/pod-product-compliance
Lightning Source LLC
Chambersburg PA
CBHW030802020726
47499CB00006B/1730